A Real Woman Knows a Real Man

A Real Woman Knows a Real Man

Nina Black

URBAN BOOKS

www.urbanbooks.net

This is a work of fiction. Any references or similarities to actual events, real people, living or dead, or to real locales are intended to give the novel a sense of reality. Any similarity in other names, characters, places, and incidents is entirely coincidental.

URBAN SOUL is published by

Urban Books
1199 Straight Path
West Babylon, NY 11704

ISBN-13: 978-1-59983-050-6
ISBN-10: 1-59983-050-7

First Printing: February 2010
10 9 8 7 6 5 4 3 2 1

Printed in the United States of America

A Real Woman
Knows a
Real Man

Chapter 1

Thirty-two-year-old Sasha Michaels loved her new position as nurse supervisor at Hope Hospital in Huntersville, Virginia. The job and her decision to return to her hometown was a nice transition as a new beginning for herself and her son, Craig. Since her return in the middle of June, she'd made new friends and reestablished an old friendship she'd left behind as a teenage bride.

During her lunch break in the employees' lounge, Sasha sat chatting with Pam. She felt a tingling in the pit of her tummy, however, when Dr. Eric Prince, dressed in blue scrubs, breezed into the room. To her, Eric Prince was a gem of a brother. He had that "it" factor. Six feet tall, he was great-looking and reeked of charisma. His complexion was a golden brown, and he had amber-colored eyes that were both heavenly and hypnotic. And Sasha was always tempted to touch, to feel the natural wave pattern and fine texture of his close-cut hair.

Dr. Prince lavished a warm smile on Sasha and Pam Hayes, the ward clerk, as he stood at the vending machine. He scooped his soda out of the bin. "Ladies, how are you this busy day?"

"We're hanging in. This week we had a baby boom," Sasha said. "The other nurses told me there was a heavy snowstorm during the months of December and January in Huntersville. Conditions were perfect for mating." She smiled.

Chuckling, Dr. Prince dropped down on the leather sofa and propped his feet up on the table, which was cluttered with old magazines and newspapers. "Yeah, it was one chilly winter. We're going to have lots of kids sharing the same birthday week," he said, looking amused. "That's for sure."

Dr. Prince took gulps of his drink, then began a conversation with Pam about her husband, whom he knew from the gym.

Sasha tuned out their conversation and focused on her private thoughts of Eric Prince, ob-gyn. Breathing deeply, she couldn't get over how self-conscious she became of her appearance when he was around. Whenever they worked together on the floor or in the delivery room, she was always rushing around in her loose pink scrubs, thinking her hair was a bit frizzled. She couldn't deny her attraction to his personality, which was a mixture of charm and arrogance. But what really turned her on was his confidence.

What woman could resist a man who knew who he was? she mused.

Sasha had heard rumors that Eric Prince wasn't about monogamy. From what she had learned, he was a love-'em-and-leave-'em kind of guy, making the rounds with all the available women in town, and quite a few at Hope Hospital. Yet his reputation didn't keep the women from wanting a chance with him, hoping they could change him and become the next Mrs. Prince.

Pam had told her that he had turned into a player as soon as the ink dried on his divorce papers. According to her, Dr. Prince had gone to the Caribbean and gotten a quickie divorce. He had found out his wife was cheating on him and made the split immediately.

Men have a way of moving on and letting go of such situations much easier and quicker than women, Sasha had thought then. It had taken her nearly three years to pull herself together from the humiliation and shame she'd endured in her marriage. Her ex-husband had remarried and begun a new family. Now she was a single mother with a fourteen-year-old son.

Since her ex-husband's wife had twin sons within the year, he hadn't had much time to devote to their son, which made him feel not wanted by his father, and left her to deal with his moodiness.

Suddenly, a nurse's aide pushed open the door, seeking Dr. Prince. "That young girl is frantic and getting loud. The nurse said she is nearly dilated and you should come."

"Here we go again. See you ladies later," Dr. Prince said, hurrying out of the room.

Pam turned to Sasha. "He's been one busy man. He delivered three babies through the night and one of those was a C-section delivery."

"Yeah, I've seen the charts. He's been here since late last night. He still has two women in labor." Sasha thought of the rounds she had made since arriving on her shift that morning.

"By the time he leaves here, he'll have to check in at his private practice. He won't have time to play with that Mia Evans. Have you heard about those two?"

"You know I haven't. I've only been here three months and I don't know many people, so I don't hear any gossip."

Pam leaned toward her. "Let me put you in the loop. Girl, it seems that Mia and Dr. Prince had a thing going on for about a month. Mia was walking around with a goofy smile on her face. I can imagine that Dr. Prince knows how to treat a woman when he is between the sheets." She laughed softly. "Anyway, Mia and Dr. Prince were having lunches together and had been seen out in clubs, hanging in darkened corners, making out like teens. Mia was bragging about what she thought she had with him. She really believed she was going to be someone special in his life, but the next thing you know,

Dr. Prince had cooled on her and directed his attention elsewhere."

"My goodness, you sure have all the info. Where in the world did you learn all of this? Is this on a hospital blog or something?" Sasha laughed softly.

"Leave me alone, girl. I have my sources. I've been here nearly five years, so I know almost everyone who works here. Believe me, at times Hope Hospital can be like a reality drama, with all the secrets of the people's personal lives. I love coming to work to see what the new episodes will be."

"You are too much. So tell me, who is Dr. Prince seeing now?" Sasha grinned.

"Well, I have a feeling it's this Dr. Gabrielle Ryan. I don't know how long that will last. She is way too serious. You'll see what I mean if you get to meet her. I don't think it'll last long. Dr. Prince likes a woman who is more down-to-earth." Pam looked Sasha in the eye. "You're mighty interested. I've got a feeling you've been smitten by his charm. And . . . you could be one of his ladies. You're attractive—the kind of woman he likes. Oh, by the way, I caught him checking you out as though you are some kind of tasty pastry." She pointed her finger and grinned. "Hey, you could be the next one on the Prince's bliss list. Look out." Then Pam burst into laughter.

Sasha's eyes widened, and she could feel the back of her neck growing warm. She didn't want to admit to Pam that just the thought of being with Eric Prince was enticing. But she didn't plan on having her emotions toyed with. Fighting back a demure grin, she said, "I hardly see that happening. I don't have time for his kind of games. I bet when he learns I have a fourteen-year-old son, it will be a major turnoff. I can't think about another man. My son is the only man I can think of for now. Not only is that boy almost as tall as I am, but he's beginning to be a handful."

"I heard that. But if I was you and Dr. Prince approached me, I sure would have dinner with him. You know who you are, Sasha. You're not desperate or flaky like most of the women he's been running through. I believe you could slow him down and give him a bit of structure to his life again. I can see you as the kind of woman he would respect, lady."

Sasha smiled at the compliment. "Well, this isn't a problem for me. He hasn't come on to me. We're only professional colleagues and nothing more."

"You're attracted to Dr. Prince. I've seen the way you smile at him and how the tone of your voice is a bit sweeter when you're talking to him. Heck, I could go for him. He is a charmer. I love those light eyes of his; they're amazing. I can hold his stare but so long," she said with a bit of humor. "He makes me almost want to forget I'm married and be one of his playmates."

Pam and Sasha burst into laughter.

"You're something else. When I do meet your husband, I'm going to tell him about your decadent thoughts."

"You wouldn't dare," Pam said, feigning fear. "Dr. Prince is fine, but no one can make me leave my sugar bear. I lucked out when I married him."

"You're lucky to be able to make it work. Marriage is hard work."

"It is. I hope you haven't given up on it because of your divorce. You're an attractive woman and should really consider giving marriage one more try."

Sasha shrugged.

"Despite all the gossip, you won't find a more caring and better doctor than Eric Prince. He has a successful private practice, and his patients all adore him. I knew Dr. Prince before he was divorced. All of this going from one woman to another is a phase, I believe. He's only trying to hide his disappointment. He dates one woman after another, and it appears you've chosen to shut your emotions down completely for men."

"Well, thank you, Oprah," Sasha teased.

Pam excused herself to go to the restroom.

Sitting alone in the lounge, Sasha knew she had done a good job of hiding the attraction and interest she had in Eric Prince. Although she was fond of him, she had no plans of flirting with him. She had no time to play the kind of games he was into at the moment. She reminded herself she had returned home to Huntersville, Virginia, and Hope Hospital for a fresh start and to place behind her all the negative emotions tied in with her ex-husband Trey's marriage and the recent birth of his twin sons. Also, Huntersville was her chance of placing her teen son in a healthy emotional environment. She believed he needed the change more than she.

The door to the lounge burst open. It was Dr. Prince. He stared at Sasha. "May I get you to assist me with this delivery? Our teen mother, Aisha, is asking for you. It seems as though you've made a bond with her."

"Sure. I don't mind. I'm done eating. I'll be right there." As he disappeared, Sasha jumped to her feet, cleared her trash, and tossed it.

Pam returned to the lounge.

"I'm going to assist Dr. Prince. That teen mother has asked for me to help with his delivery."

Just as she headed for the door, she felt her cell phone vibrate in the pocket of her uniform. She flipped the phone open and recognized the number of her son's middle school. She moaned, getting Pam's attention. "Oh my goodness. It's my son's school. I wonder what happened. Will you call this number for me and check to see if he is all right physically? Anything else, I will deal with once I'm done with the delivery."

"Sure thing," Pam said, taking down the number she saw on the phone Sasha held for her to see.

Sasha entered the delivery room and arrived in the midst of Aisha's cries of discomfort. Dr. Prince stood before the young teen, instructing her in a quiet tone. Aisha's mother, a few years younger than Sasha, stood nearby, looking helpless.

Sasha eased up beside Aisha and took her hand.

Just for a moment Aisha offered a smile of gratitude. Her face was drenched in perspiration, and her hair had become fuzzy around its edges from the restless shifting during her labor. Her smile faded and was replaced by a wince. "I need something for pain. I can't do this— I can't," Aisha moaned.

"I don't want you to fight the pushing feeling. Give in to it," Dr. Prince said as he sat on a stool between his patient's bent knees. "I can see your baby's head."

"We're getting there, Aisha," Sasha said, maintaining the grip Aisha had on her hand. "Hang in there and push, sweetie."

Squeezing her eyes tightly, Aisha strained and pushed.

"Good. Only a couple more and it will be over," Sasha told her.

Nearly every time Sasha witnessed a teen girl delivering her first child, she was taken back to the memory of the birth of her son. Then she had had only her grandmother to stand by her side. Trey, her son's father, had doubts placed in his mind by his parents as to whether or not Sasha was really carrying his baby. Trey's mother thought a girl like Sasha, whose mother had died a junkie, was up to no good and only wanted to hook up with Trey because he had a bright academic future and a burning desire to become a doctor. Though Sasha had swallowed her pride and gone to Trey's mother to assure her tearfully that the baby was indeed Trey's, his mother had turned a deaf ear to her. His mother couldn't wrap her mind around the fact that Sasha was nothing like her mother, who had a reputation of sleeping around to get money for her drugs. She had made it clear to Sasha that she didn't want her in their family. Yet once her baby was born and Trey and his family had seen the infant, all the doubts faded. Craig came out resembling the baby pictures of his father, Trey Michaels.

A loud groan from Aisha let Sasha know that the baby was coming fast. She took a seat on the bed beside her patient and placed her arm around her shoulder, urging her to sit upright to make it happen sooner.

"This is it, Aisha. We're going to do this," Sasha said. "I want you to breathe deeply and push with all your might." Sasha breathed hard and deeply, so Aisha could imitate her.

Aisha did as she was told and pressed down as hard as she could.

"You're doing great, Aisha. Keep it up. Your baby is coming." Dr. Prince smiled at his patient.

As though Aisha was her daughter, Sasha continued to coach in a caring tone. During the last big push, Aisha let loose a loud groan and gripped Sasha's hand so tightly, it ached.

When the baby emerged completely into the doctor's hand, Aisha fell back onto the bed, breathing heavily.

Sasha smiled. She took a cool cloth and wiped Aisha's face. "You did it, *Mommy*. You did a great job."

"A strong, healthy boy." Dr. Prince grinned. After clipping the umbilical cord, he laid the squealing, trembling baby on the tummy of an exhausted yet joyful Aisha.

As Sasha beamed and cooed at the baby, Eric Prince was hit by an intense feeling of admiration for his nurse. The look on her beautiful face captivated him. His heart lurched. Sasha stirred emotions within him and renewed his soul. Dr. Prince noticed her passion for nursing. The look on her face was ethereal; it was what made him want to get to know her in more than a carnal sense. His player days were over, he decided. His goal from this moment on would be to fit into Sasha's world and have her share his.

Sasha observed Aisha's teary eyes, which revealed the love and pride she felt in that first magical moment of motherhood. Sasha felt a glow of emotion in her heart. For her the miracle of childbirth never grew old. Noticing the grandmother standing with her face wet with tears, Sasha offered her a warm smile and went to bring her into the circle that was her family.

As the grandmother took hold of the infant's

hand, the anxiety melted from her face. Then she kissed and embraced her daughter, whispering endearments.

"You're a beautiful-looking family," Sasha said. "From the glow on your face, I know you're going to be a wonderful mother."

Holding her baby, Aisha stared at Sasha. "Thanks for hangin' around for me. I couldn't have done it without you."

"The pleasure was mine," Sasha said. "We're going to take the baby in a moment to clean it and have it checked by the pediatrician."

While the baby was being attended to, Dr. Prince handed Aisha's chart to Sasha and drew her into a lingering glance. When he stared at her, Sasha noticed a sparkle of admiration. She was flattered. Her heart skipped a beat; she had become mesmerized by his awesome eyes.

"Great job with Aisha. You made this delivery a lot easier. I was certain we were going to have a much harder time with her. She was so afraid of the delivery," he informed Sasha. "A few of the doctors had mentioned how good you are, especially with our young mothers. Most of the time when I get the teen moms in, we have a time. I mean, they scream and can really carry on. I wish more of the nurses had the quiet yet stern rapport with the younger ones the way you do." He patted her shoulder. "If you need me for anything else on Aisha, I can be reached in the cafeteria. I need coffee and something to eat before my other delivery begins. My next patient should be ready in a couple of hours. You want to assist me?"

"I'm going to have to leave, Dr. Prince. My son has this thing at school and—"

"No problem." He smiled and strolled from the room.

After he left, Sasha could still feel her heart racing. While she added notes to the doctor's orders, she chided herself for getting so flustered. Yet she liked the way he'd made her feel. He reminded her she was still a woman with healthy desires.

Taking a calming breath, Sasha came back to her senses. Dr. Eric Prince wasn't the man for her. Hadn't Pam told her he was in a player phase?

Once Sasha had retrieved her son from school, she was livid from the report of bad behavior the dean of students, Mrs. Parham, had relayed to her concerning Craig. Not only did Sasha have to leave work early because her son was fighting and had gotten suspended, but she also learned her son had received several in-school detentions for being disrespectful to two of his teachers. The whole revelation was humiliating to her, because Craig hadn't mentioned a word to her of his punishment or shown her the slips they had given him at school over the matter.

Then again, Sasha felt guilty, because she had been so caught up in her new job—her promotion to nursing supervisor at Hope Hospital. She couldn't remember the last time she had taken the time to really talk about school with him, and assumed that everything was going great with her fourteen-year-old.

On the drive home, Sasha peered into the rearview mirror of her car to get a glimpse of her sullen son, who'd insisted on sitting in the backseat. Craig was slumped low, as though ashamed to be seen with her, and he had an angry look to match his aloof attitude. Sasha worried he might be hanging out with the wrong crowd at school or in the neighborhood. She realized she was going to have to keep closer tabs on him and decided to start making him go to his great-grandmother's house after school.

Feeling a bit scared, she wished his father would be more involved in his life. She could love Craig, feed him, and clothe him, and do whatever it took to be a good mother, but he needed a man in his life to show him how to become a man himself.

When Sasha had left northern Virginia where Trey, her ex-husband, lived, she had selfishly vowed she wouldn't ask him for anything. Now she knew she was going to have to break that promise to get her son on the right track. Craig's well-being was more important than her pride. The first chance she got, she was going to call

Trey and remind him he had a son who required his attention as much as his new infant sons did.

She and Trey didn't do much talking. Four years ago he had remarried another doctor with a legacy of professionals in her family, the kind of woman his parents wanted for him. Sasha could imagine how thrilled Trey's mother was to have Sasha out of his life, with the jaded past of her mother, who had been fodder for gossip with her pathetic life as a drug addict. Trey's parents had moved out of Huntersville to Atlanta, Georgia, where his father had taken a job as an accountant, and Craig hadn't seen them since leaving elementary school. She could imagine that Trey's parents didn't want Craig around because they were afraid that Sasha would want to be with them too. That was far from Sasha's mind. She would have allowed Craig to visit them at his age now. She wanted him to know and love his family, whether they were from her side of the family or Trey's, and wouldn't do anything to keep him from knowing them, despite their cold treatment through the years.

Sasha knew she and Trey had gotten married only because she had gotten pregnant with Craig when she was in her teens. Trey was older, and she had needed someone to fill the void in her life after Cathy, her mother, had died from a drug overdose.

Cathy was a social worker who'd gotten involved with a man who used drugs and introduced her to them. The romance and the partying turned into a nightmare for Cathy. Slowly, she lost her grip on everything important to her. After she lost her job, she gave custody of ten-year-old Sasha to her mother. Cathy had broken her parents' heart over the way she had thrown her entire life away over a man, and a drug habit.

Sasha watched her son scramble out of the car without looking at her or saying a word after she reached her apartment complex and pulled into a parking place. She thought, *Wait until he learns, for the next week, he won't be playing any video games or listening to that iPod he keeps jammed in his ears.* Sasha planned on sending him to spend his three-day suspension with his great-grandmother, who had no extra cable stations, so there'd be no music videos for him. *He's going to have to learn how to appreciate soap operas, or pick up a book and do more reading,* she mused with satisfaction.

She reached in her purse for her keys and her cell phone, and noticed she had one missed message. She listened to the message from Pam as she walked toward her apartment.

"Hey, Sasha. I had to call you to let you know the Prince had been inquiring about you. He was interested in knowing if you were involved with anyone. The only thing I gave up was the fact you were divorced. I said nothing else. Thought you'd be interested. Talk to you later."

The message made her smile. Yes, she was flattered, but she was still going to be cautious of Dr. Prince. She hurried into her apartment to deal with her life. Craig. It was time for her to show him who was still running the household.

Chapter 2

The next morning Sasha awoke early to drive a suspended Craig to her grandmother's house. Her widowed grandma, Claudia Hill, still lived in the small three-bedroom home she and her husband, Willie, had bought back in the late 'fifties. The quiet neighborhood held good memories for Sasha, giving her comfort at a time when her mother had forsaken her.

Opening the door with the same key her grandma had given her as a teen, Sasha called to her beloved grandmother as she entered the house.

Grandma Claudia peeked around the corner of the kitchen. "Good morning, children. Come on back and get yourselves something to eat. I've cooked up plenty of breakfast. I know you and Craig are used to cold cereal and eating those nasty breakfast bars. Yuck!"

Sasha wanted to plead not guilty to her sixty-five-year-old grandmother, but didn't. She wanted her to believe she was one of those women who could have it all—a career and raising her son—without a man.

Craig entered the kitchen and greeted his great-grandmother with a kiss on her cheek. "Morning, Grand," he said, eyeing the scrambled eggs and bacon on the stove. He rushed toward the stove with a plate.

"Uh-uh. Wash those hands first, mister," Grandma Claudia chided with humor.

Sasha followed suit and joined Craig at the kitchen sink to clean her hands. "I have to admit, I am hungry this morning. Everything smells delicious, Grandma. I'm glad you cooked, but you didn't have to prepare all of this."

"I know I didn't, but I wanted to. You've got a growing boy who is skinny as a string bean. We've got to put some meat on him." She winked at Craig. "Since he's been put out of school, I intend to work him and feed him good." She took a sip of her coffee. "Yep, he's going to be a big help to me. Not only will I get my work done, but I won't have to pay anyone to do my hard chores for me."

"Sounds good to me. But you can't forget the homework he has to do as well. He has his backpack with all the assignments I gathered from his teachers."

"Don't worry, baby. We'll make time for schoolwork too." The short, small-framed woman got up from her seat to get some more coffee.

"Say what?" Craig exclaimed, frustration showing on his brown face.

"You're on punishment, young man. Did you think your grandmother was going to let you lie around and watch television, and raid her refrigerator, knowing you've been cutting up in school?"

Grandma glanced at her kitchen clock. "Son, you can have thirty minutes to watch the morning news show. That's good for you. Go on and take your plate in the living room. Right after your mom leaves for work, the television gets turned off. We're going to get busy. You and I have a big day before us."

Looking sullen, Craig did as he was told, mumbling his dissatisfaction to himself.

"I know you aren't talking. What was that you said?" Sasha said with a tone that dared him to repeat what he said.

Grinning, Grandma squeezed Sasha's arm. "Let him be. I bet he won't get suspended again once we're done with him these next three days."

"I certainly hope not." Sasha set her plate on the table and took a seat.

"Have you heard anything from his daddy?"

"It's been a while. I would love for Trey to show more interest in his life, but since he's remarried and had those twin baby boys, it seems as though he's forgotten he has a teen son."

"That's a shame. What's wrong with these men today? Why can't they learn to spread their love the way a woman does?"

"I blame Trey's neglect for Craig's behavior. He's been through a lot in the last few years— the divorce between his father and me, accepting the fact that his father was marrying Regina, and the birth of their twins. Then my decision to move and accept the promotion here to make a fresh start for us couldn't have been easy for him either, leaving his friends and the area where he grew up. I expected there to be some adjustment problems, stuff I could handle. I never imagined him to become aggressive in school. That's just not like him."

"Yes, indeed, the child has been through some changes. He's going to be fine, though. You had your issues to deal with, growing up, but you survived. I know you were confused and hurt by how your mother lived, but it didn't keep you from maintaining your self-respect."

"That was because you and Granddad taught me to hold my head up. You always reminded me that Mom's problem wasn't mine. In spite of her inability to care for me, you taught me to love and respect her. I have to admit, it was hard, but the older I got, the more I saw how Mom was struggling with her drug problem."

As silence fell between the two, Sasha's mind suddenly turned to happier times she had had with her mother. She remembered how pretty, lively, and ambitious she was before her addiction changed her into a spiritually and physically broken woman, and the overdose that killed her.

Through it all, Sasha had prayed for a change, but the change never came.

Sasha noticed her grandmother's eyes had grown dewy, and the pained expression filled her eyes when there was talk of her only daughter.

Grandma Claudia pressed her lips together as she seized Sasha's hand, closing her eyes briefly, fighting her heartache. Glancing upward and then at her granddaughter, she said, "Child support . . . is Trey keeping up with that?"

Holding on to her Grandma's loving hand, Sasha caressed it and offered a smile, to ease the discomfort of the memories of her mother the two would always share. "No trouble with that. My problem is with him giving Craig time and attention."

"That's priceless. Craig deserves those things from his father. After the way he betrayed you, humiliated you all through your marriage, I know you don't want to have to deal with him any more than you must."

"You know I don't."

"But you're going to have to set all your issues with Trey aside for the love of your son. You and Trey are going to have to come together for Craig's sake. We can't allow another soul in our family to get lost on the wrong path. One is too much," Grandma said, her voice cracking. "There's nothing more heartbreaking than losing a child and then to lose that person to what's wrong in life. Your mother has been gone for years, but I still struggle with my pain. Your poor grandfather was devastated. I don't believe he ever made peace with it before he died."

"Grandma, please . . . let's remember the good. Remember you were the one who kept me strong and told me we had to move on and cling to what was good about Mom. And that's the way I try to remember her."

Reaching out and palming Sasha's face, Grandma said, "Your mother would be so proud of you. She did love you, Sasha. When you were born and she looked at your cherub face, she was smitten. You've become everything she used to dream for you—pretty, bright, ambitious, and strong. I'm so thrilled you got that job at Hope Hospital. The older people in this neighborhood all take pride in you too. They know the struggle you had to get where you are."

Breathing deeply to ease her mixed emotions, Sasha knew she had to go before she'd be in tears. That was the last thing she needed to do to begin her day. "It's getting late, Grandma. I should be on my way to the hospital before it gets too late." She jumped to her feet and picked up her plate of half-eaten food and set it in the sink. "Craig."

Craig loped to the doorway of the kitchen, where he stood with his hands jammed in his jeans pockets. "What, Mom?"

"I don't want you to give your grand any trouble. You got me?"

He gave her a half grin that reminded her of Trey.

"Mom, you ain't got to worry. I ain't messing with Grand. I know she don't play." He looked at his grand and laughed, then returned to the living room.

"He's a mess." Grandma Claudia shook her head, showing her amusement. "Go on. Don't worry a bit over him." She stood and followed Sasha to the front door. "Have a good day at work, precious," she said, reaching in for Sasha to share a kiss the way they always did when they parted.

"Love you. I'll call you guys on one of my breaks later today." Sasha hustled out the door and to her car in the crisp autumn air to go off to do her shift at Hope Hospital.

Sasha strolled up the hallway to the nurses' station, where Pam Hayes was busy at the computer and getting things in order for the day.

After the usual morning chitchat, Pam leaned close to Sasha, who was checking out the charts of the new patients in the ward and those who would be checking out soon. She said, "Dr. Prince is here, making his rounds. He asked me what time you were due for your shift."

Glancing at Pam, Sasha struggled to hide her delight. "He probably wants to discuss his patients' care with me the way he always does." She shrugged and continued going through her charts.

"I'm sure this is more than professional, Sasha. The look in his eyes didn't speak work to me, okay? The man has a thing for you."

"Pam, are you trying to relive high school with your assumptions? Enough, okay? I'm not going there."

"I happen to think going there with him wouldn't be so bad. Live a little. Have a little fun. I'm sure you can handle him." There was a challenge in Pam's voice. "I've known Eric Prince longer than you. Prepare yourself for a social invitation of some kind."

"From what you've told me about his reputation with women, I don't have anything to get excited over."

"Shh! He's coming up the hall," Pam said, focusing on her computer.

"Ms. Michaels, good morning." Dr. Prince stood near Sasha and smiled down at her. "Did Pam tell you I've been asking for you?"

"Hi. Yes, she did. What can I do for you, Doctor?" Sasha met his gaze and waited for him to continue his conversation.

"May I have a few moments of your time? I have something I would like to speak to you about." He placed his hands behind his back in a professional manner.

Sasha could feel her face coloring from the intensity of his gaze. "I have some time now."

"Great. Let's go to the employees' lounge; it should be relatively empty now." Dressed in khaki Dockers and a green pullover shirt, he led the way down the hall and to the lounge with a swagger of confidence.

Sasha imagined he would be heading off to his private practice after he had this talk with her. Sure enough the lounge was empty, and the only sound was a morning talk show on the television.

Folding his long form onto a chair at one of the tables, Eric Prince pointed to the other seat across from him. "I'm glad I caught you this morning." He placed his well-manicured hands flat on the table and leaned toward her.

"What's this about, Doctor? I sure wouldn't like to think this has anything to do with my performance at the hospital in the last few months."

"In a way it does," he said, settling back in his chair, crossing one leg over the other. He stared at her intensely.

Sasha was bothered by the way he studied her. Surely, there was nothing negative he could say about her work. She had given one hundred ten percent of herself to her duties.

"Don't worry. Believe me, everyone who has the opportunity to work with you has nothing but positive comments of you. As for myself, I've been quite impressed with you as well."

His words created a look of relief.

"I asked you here to see if I could recruit you to work at the Hope Hospital Free Clinic. We sure could use a nurse of your caliber there. Once you have a chance to check out the program, I'm sure you'll enjoy the work we do. I've seen how good you are with the patients here. The women adore being cared for by you. At the clinic not only do we deal with women and maternity patients, but we care for a lot of senior citizens and people in the area with chronic conditions such as high blood pressure and diabetes. The clinic is located in the inner city of Huntersville at a strip mall on Segar Street. The hospital has a grant from the government that funds it. The pay will not be as much as you get here, but it's enough to be appreciated." He held her gaze. "I find it quite fulfilling to work there, and I'm sure you will too. I want to be a part of the organization. There's no doubt in my mind, if you decide to be a part of the staff, you will be an asset."

Flattered by his compliment and confidence in her, Sasha was at a momentary loss for words. She decided the clinic was something she would love being a part of. Yet she had her son to consider too. She would have to speak to her grandmother to see if she would have the time to help her with Craig whenever she had duty at the clinic.

"I'd like to have some time to think this over. It does sound interesting, though, and most definitely something worth my while."

"I can respect that. I'd like an answer in a week. How's that?"

"Perfect."

He stood to let her know he was done. "Listen,

why don't you come to Dre's Bar and Grill on Friday evening? That's where most of the staffers from the clinic chill when the last shift is done around ten o'clock. If you stop by, I can introduce you to some of the great guys and gals you'll be working with. We have some good times at Dre's—drinking beer, talking, telling lies, and playing pool." He lavished her with a warm gaze.

That look in his eyes along with his striking good features made him even more scintillating. "Thanks. I'm going to try to drop by, Dr. Prince."

"Please call me *Eric*," he insisted in a friendly tone. "I won't hold you any longer. I know you have rounds to make, and I've got patients waiting on me at my office." He smiled. "Have a good day."

As he made his way out of the lounge, Sasha caught the fresh clean scent of him. He didn't have the usually antiseptic smell he carried when he was on duty, delivering babies, but instead he smelled of a heady yet light expensive men's cologne that was enticing. She remained seated for a while and savored the moment.

Her spirits lifted, Sasha was sure she'd be walking on air for the rest of the day. Heading toward the nurses' station, she watched an anxious Pam rise from her computer chair and lean on the counter, her brown face full of curiosity.

"What was that all about? He left here with a sparkle in his eyes and a brand-new stride. And your face is glowing like I've never seen before. You got to tell me what happened in that lounge."

Sasha only grinned and picked up the charts she'd left behind. "I have work to do, and so do you." She wanted to torture Pam. She made her way down to the end of the maternity hallway to begin rounds. As she walked, she heard Pam calling her in a humorous hushed tone. Sasha turned in her direction and placed a finger over her lips to silence her and gave her a big, mischievous grin before she vanished into one of the rooms. She would keep her friend guessing until she saw she couldn't bear it anymore.

Chapter 3

Sasha had a five o'clock Friday hair appointment at the Style Salon, a beauty parlor owned by her close friend, Crystal Forbes. Entering the parlor, Sasha found the place as busy as it always was on a Friday evening. As usual the television was too loud, and the customers chattered, giggled, and laughed from all the latest dish in the community. Thankfully, Crystal had just finished with a customer, so Sasha didn't have to wait in the reception area.

Sasha looked at her friend. "You're still going with me to Dre's Bar and Grill, aren't you?"

Crystal placed a hand on her size-fourteen hip. "I sure am. I'm glad you have somewhere for us to go tonight. Greg and I are still on the outs. Maybe I can find myself someone new. Girl, I'm so tired of that man." She draped a towel around Sasha's neck and led her to the shampoo bowl.

"I'm glad you have an interest in getting out of the house. I was beginning to worry about you. I know you got needs. You've got to find yourself a good man."

With her head back on the rim of the sink, Sasha looked up at Crystal and frowned as she began to suds her hair. "I'm not on the prowl for a man. I've got too much pride for that. Besides, I've got too much going on in my life to be fooling with these unpredictable men who are available. I'm still getting readjusted to Huntersville and all the changes it made in the years I've been away. And I'm trying to keep Craig in line. Did I tell you he got suspended three days for fighting in school?"

"Not my baby Craig. I can't believe that." Crystal massaged the shampoo through Sasha's hair in a relaxing manner.

"Well, he's in middle school. And he's the new kid. You know how that can be. I suppose he feels as though he has to prove himself as a man, so to speak."

Crystal grunted with understanding. "Knowing you, you've got him on punishment."

"You'd better believe it. I've got him staying with my grandmother instead of leaving him home alone where it would be more like a vacation."

"If Miss Claudia got him, mercy on him." Crystal laughed softly. "She is going to work his nerves so badly, that poor Craig will think twice before he acts." She chuckled. "Remember how she kept tabs on us when we were his age? If your grandma saw me out and I wasn't being the lady she thought I should be, she would check me on the spot right in front of anyone. Miss Claudia does not play."

"That's exactly why his narrow behind is with her. I've been too tired to really discipline him the way I should, but once he gets a taste of the old-school ways I was raised on, he'll be back on track."

"I heard that. Now about tonight. Did you say that we weren't just going to chill, that it had something to do with a job?"

"It does. You see, Dr. Prince—Eric—invited me. He wants me to work at the Free Clinic on Segar Street that he supervises. He told me most of the staff hangs out at Dre's on Friday evenings to relax and let off some steam. He wants me to meet some of them, so I can come to a decision about whether I'd like to work there."

"Oh, Dr. Prince. I've seen and heard a lot of good things about him from the ladies here. They all adore him, girl. He is a fine brother, with a capital *F*. He and his fraternity brothers worshipped at our church one Sunday. After the service, all of the ladies thought they were in heaven with Dr. Prince and all the handsome professional men who had come along with him. We served dinner after worship. You should have seen the single women, making sure those men had a plate, and their company, to make them feel welcomed."

Sasha laughed at the way Crystal related the incident.

"You heard me speak of Pam from work? The one who knows everybody's business?"

"Yeah, I have."

"Well, she told me he comes from a wealthy family. He's lived a silver-spoon life. Yet you wouldn't know, from his down-to-earth personality. I find him downright irresistible. And his eyes, oh my stars, Crystal, they're amber colored. I swear, you can get hypnotized, if you aren't careful."

Rinsing warm water through Sasha's hair, Crystal said, "Sounds to me as though somebody wants to get to know this man a lot better than a working relationship."

Sasha didn't mean to be so transparent, but Crystal had been her friend forever and she knew her secret would be safe with her. She smiled to let Crystal know she was interested in Eric Prince.

"This is the best news I've had in a while. I'd like to see you with someone like him." Crystal chortled. "Heck, I've been praying for you to allow another man to get close to you. You've been too closed off since your divorce. It's time for you to enjoy life again."

"Maybe I'm more ready now. I had to give myself time to get over the humiliation and disappointment over the way I could never make my marriage work the way I felt it should. No matter how insensitive or thoughtless my ex was,

I always held on to a glimmer of hope that everything would change, so he and I could make a happy home for Craig."

"I hear you. I'm a survivor of one divorce and now a failed live-in relationship." Crystal rubbed a lavender-scented conditioner through Sasha's hair and then rinsed. "Okay, go to my chair so I can make you glamorous. You're going to be gorgeous for when you see your man."

"I was thinking I could have some curls. I'd like for my hair to be fluffy and loose."

"Ooowee!" Crystal exclaimed. "I got you. We're going to work it out. I'm going to set your hair and place you under the dryer. Don't worry about a thing."

Settling into her seat, Sasha said, "I'm glad you're going with me tonight. It makes it a lot easier for me to face Eric this evening. I still want to play it cool with him. I can't let him know I have feelings yet."

"You don't have to explain to me. I'm looking forward to going to Dre's. I understand the atmosphere is a lot better since they got new management. Now they cater to a more professional and business-minded, mid-twenty-something-and-beyond crowd. So the time you spend under my hot dryer is going to be worthwhile."

Crystal volunteered to pick Sasha up at her place that evening. The moment she saw Sasha in the plain shirt she'd chosen, she told her she looked like she was going to a church picnic.

Crystal went into Sasha's closet and came up with a glitzy blue off-the-shoulder number with the price tag still on it. "You must have had a night like this in mind when you bought this one," she said, tickled over the ideal find. She thrust it at Sasha. "Change into this, and get rid of that big old-fashioned bra and put on a strapless bra."

Pretending to be peeved, Sasha snatched the top and went into her bathroom to dress. In a moment, she returned for Crystal's approval, twirling like a model. "How is this?"

Crystal eyed her friend. "That's a big improvement. You look sexy. All we need are some bigger earrings. I have some in my purse. I knew you wouldn't have anything but those small cutesy hoops you wear all the time. Now sit on the bed, so I can add a touch more makeup to your face. What am I going to do with you?" Crystal sighed. "You used to be so into fashion and makeup. You were the one who taught me how to glam it up. Those years of marriage to Trey stunted your growth as a woman."

"Yes, it did take a toll on me, but I'm working hard to shake off all the negative energy. I want to be the best woman I can be, with a spirit no man can break."

"Now you're talking."

* * *

It was a little past eleven o'clock when the ladies entered the festive and lively Dre's Bar and Grill.

Strutting on four-inch heels she hadn't worn in quite some time, Sasha grew self-conscious. She began to regret having Crystal talk her into the outfit she wore. She plastered a smile on her face to hide her insecurity.

"I like this spot," Crystal gushed, panning all the interesting-looking men. "You can have your doctor and any other man you want, with all the fineness in here." She leaned close to Sasha's ear. "You want to see if you can find that Prince, so we can all get a table?"

"I'm looking, but there are no signs of him."

"I'm looking too, but not for your man. Mercy, it's like a candy store, Sasha."

Eric had been at the bar with his friend Miles Rollins, sharing drinks and listening to him talk of his troubled relationship. Bored with Miles's reasons for not letting his girlfriend talk him into marriage, Eric lost his focus. He'd been eyeing the entrance, wondering if Sasha was going to make it. Not only did he want her to meet the staffers from the clinic, but he also wanted to see her and have a chance to talk to her outside of work.

"I'm not ready for a lifetime commitment with her," Miles continued. "Rene and I have taken our relationship as far as we can. Living with her for two years has only shown me that I'm not meant to be her husband."

"In that case, you should man up and tell her, and move out. All the foolish games you two play are ridiculous. Every time things get out of hand and heated, you end up sleeping over at my crib. In fact, I'm considering asking you to meet me halfway on my household expenses." He chuckled.

"Ha-ha! Can't you be quiet and listen?" Miles looked pensive. "I don't know where it all went wrong. Rene and I had great chemistry in the bedroom. At one time, she and I couldn't get enough of each other. The fire is gone because Rene has too much mouth, and she has become a detective. 'Where've you been? Who were you with? I heard this, I heard that.'" He shrugged. "What kind of stuff is that? And, to top if off, if she thinks I'm lying, she punishes me by cutting me off from sex. She's cruel with hers too. She'll take a shower in her sweet-smelling stuff and crawl into bed naked and dare me not to touch her. She thinks these antics will get me to marry her?"

"It's time to move on. The sooner the better."

Miles ordered another drink and wiped his hand over his face wearily. "I hate breakups. Rene is going to be a drama queen. I'm talking the possibility of slashed tires, broken windshields, and who knows what else, with her hot temper."

Eric patted him on the shoulder. "Don't worry, brother. You've got that good car insurance. I'll be watching your back as much as you will. Come on and move in with me, so you get on with your life. You won't be able to move back into your house for another year. I don't know why you rented to that military family for two years."

"I thought Rene and I were going to make a home." Miles shook his head. He sighed with resignation. "I always screw up big time, don't I? And drama always finds me." He chortled.

"You keep dealing with the same kind of crazy women over and over again."

"It looks that way, doesn't it?" Miles finished off the remainder of his drink.

Before Eric could say anything more, he caught a glimpse of Sasha with another woman. The two of them stood midway in the large room amidst the crowd. He figured Sasha was trying to get sight of him.

Instead of going for her, he stood and took her in. She looked marvelous to him as he sized up the shape of her body in figure-hugging jeans and the sassy glittery blouse that adorned her form. The sneakers she usually wore were replaced by hot-looking pumps, which made her body shapelier and rock seductively whenever she took a step.

"Miles, we'll talk more later about this. That honey I told you about has arrived. I'm going to greet her. Find a table for four. She has a girlfriend with her. Since your relationship is cooling, maybe her friend can bring you some cheer."

He hurried away from the bar and worked his way through the crowd to Sasha.

"Your Prince is coming our way," Crystal murmured to Sasha.

Hearing this, Sasha stood straight and looked in the direction of Crystal's playful expression.

"Sasha, I was beginning to think you had changed your mind," Eric said, taking her hand and giving her a friendly embrace. "I'm glad you made it."

His nearness made her heart swell. "I've been looking forward to a night out. I even brought a friend with me." She smiled. "This is Crystal Forbes. Crystal, this is Dr. Eric Prince."

"Hi. Please call me *Eric*." He extended his hand to Crystal.

"Nice to meet you, Eric."

"Come on with me," he urged the two ladies. "My friend Miles and I have a table."

Without hesitation, Eric took Sasha's hand and led her through the crowd, Crystal trailing, to a booth near the window in the middle of the place. He introduced Miles and Crystal to each other.

After Eric saw how good Miles and Crystal hit it off, he placed his hands on Sasha's waist and excused himself, so he could take her to the back rec room, where the staff from the clinic were.

Sasha felt at ease with the staffers' warmth. She had seen most of them around the hospital but hadn't had the opportunity to get to know them. Many of them raved about how much they loved working with Eric, and encouraged her to become a part of their family.

After they had watched the crew from the clinic play a couple of games of pool, Eric suggested they have drinks at the bar, where they could talk further before joining Crystal and Miles.

"It looks as though Miles and Crystal are getting along as though they've always known each other," Eric said, checking out the two.

Sasha did notice Crystal had turned up her charm and looked as though she was having the time of her life with the brother. Dark and athletic-looking, Miles was definitely the type Crystal would go for. And Sasha was certain his deep, sensual voice would be a turn-on for her too.

"I guess you can tell my friend is shy." She laughed.

"From what I've seen of her, she is far from that." Eric leaned on the bar and signaled for the bartender. "What would you like to drink?"

"I'd really like a cold beer," she said, noticing how Eric eyed her as though he hadn't seen her before. Seeing the appreciative look he gave her, the fresh hairdo and makeup proved to have been worth her time.

"Two beers here," Eric called to the bartender. He whirled his stool to face her. "What do you think of the people you met?"

"They're great. I believe I would enjoy working with them."

"I figured you'd fit in with them." He stared at her, giving her one of his wonderful grins.

Meeting his gaze and staring into his compelling eyes, she knew she had made her decision. How could she turn down an opportunity to work with him? The more she knew him, the more things she found to like about him. Also, she admired the passion he had for the clinic, and she always found working for the community rewarding.

The bartender brought their drinks in chilled mugs.

"So, can I consider you a part of my staff?"

She smiled at him. "I would say yes. If I say no, I feel as though I'll be missing out on something special."

Eric beamed. "That's great. You are really going to make our staff even more special. Don't worry about your schedule. I'm going to make it as flexible as I can, to suit your other responsibilities. I wouldn't want to interfere in your personal relationships."

"Fine. Oh, I'm single. The only person I have to answer to is my fourteen-year-old son, but my grandmother is more than willing to fill in for me with him."

Eric was pleased to hear Sasha was single, yet surprised at the age of her child. "You got a kid that's fourteen?"

"Yes, I do." She sat a bit taller and hoped he wouldn't say anything to offend her.

"That's interesting."

She shrugged. "I was a teen mother who married right out of high school," she said, searching his face for judgment of her situation.

Eric gulped some of his beer. "A teenage mother and marriage, huh? That must have been one experience for you."

Sasha caught an empathetic look in his eyes and decided to be candid with him. She was in no way ashamed of being the mother of a fourteen-year-old at thirty-two.

"It wasn't that big of a deal at eighteen. I was in love, and what happened was in the name of love. At the time my boyfriend and I couldn't relate to the disappointment his parents and my grandparents had. He and I believed we could take on the world because we were in love, and that would be enough for everything." Sasha took a drink from her beer before adding, "My grandparents, who practically raised me, weren't pleased with the turn my life had taken, yet they stood by me and my husband, who was a sophomore in college with the ambition of being a physician. Though I was young and married, my grandmother made sure I still had the opportunity to attend college and become a nurse. I attended the local college here in Huntersville, and my husband maintained his scholarship at Howard University. The long-distance relationship was hard, but I had this wide-eyed optimism that everything was going to work out for the best for us. Unfortunately, the responsibility of being a wife, raising a child, finances, and trying to make passing grades in college made our marriage one big mess.

"Once I became a nurse, I went to live with him in northern Virginia so he could complete his medical training. When he began to practice, our idealistic world had crumbled in more ways than one. He and I were never on the same page. We spent less and less time working on our marriage and a lot of time arguing." Sasha turned thoughtful. "My husband had fallen for someone new, another doctor he'd done his residency training with. He claimed she made him happier than he'd been in years.

"By that time, there wasn't much left of our marriage but the love we had for our young son. I was miserable and depressed. I knew it was time to let go of the dream of the perfect marriage for us, so we divorced. He has remarried and has begun a new family. He and his wife just had twin sons." Sasha forced a smile. "I moved here with my son for the promotion at Hope Hospital and to put my past behind me."

Without looking at Eric, she drank her beer, wondering if he would view her as a failure, now that she had shared her life with him.

Touching her on the shoulder, Eric said, "You've been through the storm, but you have so much to look forward to now that you've returned to Huntersville. I've been through a divorce, and I've experienced all the negative feelings you have. That whole scene has a way of diminishing you and causing you to do things you wish you could take back. We're only human, and all of us are searching for happiness with a new beginning."

"You can say that again." Sasha smiled.

Eric reached over, covered her hand, and squeezed it. In the dimly lit grill, he found her stunning. His fingers ached to touch the sheen and soft texture of her appealing hairdo.

Meeting his gaze, Sasha felt an eager affection coming from him. She saw a hint of smolder in those wonderful amber eyes of his, and her heart tripped a couple of paces faster. Feeling awkward, she withdrew her hand.

"Let's join Miles and Crystal. They look as though they're having fun. I'd like to order something to eat too." She slid off the stool and made her way over to Miles and Crystal.

After the group had enjoyed a meal of chicken wings and cheesy fries with plenty of cold beer, not to mention plenty of interesting conversation and laughter, it was nearly 2:00 A.M., way past Sasha's usual bedtime. By this time, Sasha had grown mellow and a bit drowsy from the tasty food and drink she had overindulged in.

Eric and Miles walked the ladies to Crystal's car. Miles and Crystal strolled to the driver's side of her car to say their good-byes, leaving Eric and Sasha on the passenger side.

"I'm glad I came this evening. I can't remember the last time I had such a great time." Sasha leaned against the car and placed her hands inside her jacket. With Eric close beside her and standing in a manner that allowed the lights on the parking lot to illuminate his features, Sasha thought he looked sexy, even downright romantic-looking.

"I'm glad you decided you'd work at the clinic. You're going to like the working conditions and the staff."

Sasha knew there would be no regrets. She looked forward to seeing him more often. Still, in the back of her mind, there was the business of him being a player. *There was no evidence of that this evening*, she thought. He had given her his undivided attention. She had ignored the fact that several women had come over to speak to him, and had seen no flirting from him. He had been nothing but a gentleman with her.

"I'm looking forward to the experience."

"Let's go, lady," Crystal called, climbing into the car.

Sasha made a motion to get into the car, placing her hand on the handle. "Well, I guess it's good night. Thanks for a great evening."

Eric's hand covered hers. "Allow me," he said.

He was standing so close to her, his voice vibrated in her ear and sent a pleasant tingle through her. She removed her hand, allowing him the privilege.

In the next moment, Eric placed a tender kiss on her face. Then he opened the car door.

Sasha turned to him and studied him, unable to say anything. Glancing at him with a nervous smile, she got inside the car. "See you later," she said in a voice that was barely audible.

"Looking forward to that," Eric said, closing the door.

As Crystal started the car, Sasha waved. With Eric watching her leave, his tender expression hit her like a wave of magic, and Sasha's closed heart bloomed with fondness for the man. It took everything in her not to look over her shoulder to take one final look at him.

On the ride home, Crystal began blabbering about how interesting Miles was, how much she liked him. Sasha pretended to listen, but she was too busy reliving every word spoken, every look, every touch she'd experienced with Eric Prince. She liked the positive vibe that hummed through her body from the time they'd spent together. She wanted to maintain her cool, see if he would give up his player ways for her.

Chapter 4

That evening when Eric left Sasha, he knew he was going to have to clear his life of anyone who might stand in the way of him getting with Sasha Michaels. That one night talking with her convinced him she was the one for him.

He reached the parking lot of his condo and saw Mia Evans's car parked in her usual spot. Up until now, she and he had had a "friends-with-benefits" relationship. Mia even had a key to his condo and would wait for him in bed. He wasn't that guy anymore. He was ready to put those ways in the past and be a better man. He was done with using sex as a means to cope with the bitterness he experienced from his divorce.

Thinking over all the women he had been through because of the issues he had from his ex-wife not appreciating him, he was consumed with shame. This phase of his life had only been a temporary relief because, no matter who he'd been with, no one could help him eradicate his feelings of loneliness, his insecurities. Yet the moment Sasha's smile warmed him and he had shared an open conversation with her, he was comforted. Her quiet personality and grace made him feel as though there was hope for him to know real intimacy once more.

Mia Evans, showing off her nipples in a T-shirt two sizes too small and a pair of thong panties, hopped off the sofa to greet him. "I was wondering what time you were coming home." She looped her arms around his neck and tiptoed to kiss Eric, but he was indifferent.

Eric kissed her on the forehead, moved out of her embrace, and headed for the kitchen. He knew he was going to have to end the thing he had with her, not wanting to have meaningless sex with her anymore. Even before this night, he had made up his mind to end it with her. He could sense that the agreement they had made for only sex was becoming clouded with Mia, and that she wanted more of a commitment from him.

Mia came up behind him. "What's wrong, Eric?"

He went to the fridge and pulled out a cold bottle of water. "You and I have to talk." He pointed to the kitchen table.

"Talk? I don't want to do that. I've been lying around most of the evening thinking of what I want you to do to me."

"Mia, will you sit down?"

"You are grumpy." Mia plopped down in the

chair across from him. "What in the world are you going through?"

"I'm not going to draw this out. You and I are done."

Mia bolted from her seat and began to pace. "Done? You can't be serious."

"I am serious. We have gone on way too long with this thing we have."

Mia glowered at him. "You've met someone new, haven't you?"

"This is about you and me, Mia. I'm not that guy who wants or needs to have a sex buddy anymore. It's time for me to get serious about my life and my career. The way I've been acting in the last few years is not the way I wish to live anymore."

Mia gave him a look of doubt. "So, basically, what you're telling me is you're giving up sex?" She laughed nervously.

He scowled at her. "No, I'm not giving that up. Let's just say I'm looking for a more meaningful relationship."

"You and I have been kickin' it for nearly three months. You and I have had some adventurous and hot times. You've been giving me the impression that it's been more than sex between us." Mia looked downcast. "I was hopeful that your feelings had become more serious, because I have fallen in love with you."

A heavy silence hung between them.

Eric got up and stood at the sink, resting his back against the counter. "When we first hooked up, I laid the rules out to you. It was supposed to be nothing but fun and games between us."

"And it was," Mia said, her voice quivering with emotion. "I couldn't help the way my feelings took over."

Eric crossed his legs. He began to rub his chin, shutting out Mia's presence.

Mia rushed up to him and pressed her well-shaped body to his. She touched his chin and leveled his face, so he could see the tears in her eyes. Brushing her body against his, she attempted to engage him in a kiss. "You know you still want me," she whispered seductively.

Eric took hold of her shoulders and held her away. "This isn't going to work. I want you to get your things together and leave."

"You're just going to throw me out in the middle of the night? Thought you would let me wait until morning." Her eyes widened with fury.

"Okay, you can stay the night, but I'm leaving. When I return in the morning, I want you to get all of your things out. And leave my key on the dresser in my bedroom. This is over." He walked past her.

Mia caught up to him and snagged his wrist. Huffed up with anger, she said, "Damn you, Eric Prince! How can you be so cold? Whenever we were together in your bed, I could swear you were feeling me in more ways than one. I was only giving you time to say that you wanted me."

He wrenched his hand out of her grip and said through clenched teeth, "I never made any promises to you, Mia. It has never been anything but sex between us, and that's all it could ever have been."

Mia felt as though he had hit her physically, shattering her dreams of them being a happily married couple. She'd been warned by her friends that Eric would never take her seriously, but she took her chances and became what he wanted her to be—pleasure between the sheets.

"Good-bye," he said in an apologetic tone, heading out the door.

"This isn't good-bye!" she screamed. "I'm not giving up on you. You have someone else. I'm going to find out who it is."

Eric thought of Sasha and how badly he wanted to win her trust. The last thing he needed was a drama diva wrecking what he wanted to build with her. He whirled around. "Stay out of my life, Mia. Let's be civil about this. This doesn't have to be a battle of wills."

"This isn't over," Mia said, arms akimbo. "You're gonna want me back. No one can satisfy you the way I can. I'm the woman for you and deep in your heart, you know it."

Eric threw his hands up in frustration. Growing tired of her tirade, he walked out of his apartment to get away from her. He was glad that part of his life was over. Never again would he use sex so casually. He had learned in his two years of playing around that there had to be love to have a meaningful relationship. Sex by itself only left one feeling lonely and worthless.

Chapter 5

Once Sasha began to work at the Hope Hospital Free Clinic in Huntersville, she and Eric developed a cozy friendship. Even though the clinic was often busy, the working conditions couldn't have been better. The staff was like a family and had no qualms about doing whatever was necessary to get the work done for the day and to meet the needs of the patients.

One Friday Crystal Forbes called to let her know she wouldn't be able to pick her up from work. She had a personal emergency. Sasha told Crystal she would call her grandmother to come for her.

Sasha hung up the phone, unaware that Eric was standing behind her. She turned toward the sound of his voice and found him scribbling on a chart, which he then placed on the desk.

"You still haven't gotten your car out of the shop yet?" Eric folded his strong arms.

"Unfortunately not. The service station has promised me I can get it tomorrow." Sasha picked up the charts of the last two patients for the evening.

"You don't have to call your grandmother. I'd be more than happy to give you a lift home. There's no need to get your grandmother out on a cold, rainy night like this. Shame on you for not thinking of me first." He smiled.

"I didn't want to bother you. I figured you had plans on a Friday evening, even if it's a rainy night."

"You're never a bother, Sasha. I'd be pleased to take you home, to your house, that is."

"I'd really appreciate it, Doctor. Thanks." Sasha's eyes lingered on his a bit longer than usual. She grinned coyly and then went and got the next patient.

While she was in the exam room, doing the vitals on the older male patient who was wheezing and had a bad cough, she couldn't help but feel a bit of excited anticipation, knowing Eric was taking her home.

Because it was a Friday and Craig was spending the night at Grandma Claudia's, Sasha was considering asking Eric up to her apartment for the first time to share a drink and to listen to some music since she would be alone at home. He'd said he had no plans, so she was going to use this chance to be alone with him.

People had noticed Eric's behavior toward

Sasha, and it was starting a buzz. Pam had mentioned to Sasha that the women he used to play with were confused over the way he'd changed and was trying to be more of an upright guy instead of the fun-loving bedmate they'd been accustomed to. They suspected there was a new woman and were curious to know who it was.

Pam claimed she had kept her mouth shut, but Sasha wondered if Pam could manage such a feat. She knew how much Pam loved to be the first to dish the latest. As far as Sasha was concerned, Pam had nothing to really discuss concerning her and Eric. Yet.

At the end of the evening shift, Eric sat at his desk making notes on charts, leaving instructions for the physician in charge of the morning opening of the clinic. Hearing Sasha moving around, refilling supplies in the exam rooms, he was glad he had given the receptionist the night off to celebrate her birthday with her boyfriend. He liked the idea of him and Sasha being the last two people in the place. Having her work with him was like having a beautiful flower around him to lift his spirits. And the more he saw of her, the more he couldn't resist fantasizing about her.

Although Sasha wore mostly loose uniforms to work, he knew that beneath the shapeless outfits, she had the body of a goddess. He had really checked her out the night she had come to Dre's Bar and Grill. Her long, loose hair, the painted-on jeans that revealed the delicious curve of her bottom, and the fancy top clinging to her ample breasts had been etched in his brain.

Feeling himself becoming aroused by his thoughts, he stood and moved about his office to clear his mind. He went to the window and peeked out the blinds to check out the weather. The rain hadn't let up any. He sighed softly. It was a perfect night for lovers to snuggle in bed and make reckless love while the rain beat upon the bedroom window, providing an ideal symphony for sexual intimacy.

Eric had the reputation of always having a woman around to fulfill his needs, but he hadn't had a woman in nearly a month. He blamed Sasha's charm and allure for that. That one evening she had come to meet with him had shown him what he wanted in a woman.

What attracted him most to Sasha along with her personality was the bit of sadness that dwelled in her eyes. She made him want to be her hero and to replace that sadness with joy. He hadn't had the opportunity to really talk with her or to be alone. Still, he could see from the way she carried herself and the things she said in the few conversations they had that she was a real woman without any agenda. The kind he thought no longer existed.

Interrupting his thoughts, Sasha said, "Is there anything else you want me to give attention to before we leave?"

"I'm sure you've covered everything thoroughly.

Let's get out of here," he said, straightening his desk without meeting her eyes, afraid that she would see the desire he had for her.

Dressed in their coats and reaching the front door, they saw that the rain had started to pour so hard they could barely see.

"We'd better wait a moment or two. If we leave now, we'd both be drenched by the time we get to my car." Eric leaned against the glass door and studied outside.

Standing close to him, Sasha said, "If I was home, I'd find this rainy night relaxing. I'd be curled up in my bed with the TV off and with a good book to keep me company."

"I can think of something I'd like to do on a rainy night, and it wouldn't be reading." He laughed softly.

"With the reputation you have, I can imagine what you'd have in mind."

"It happens to be one of the things that turns me on, especially with the right woman. Please don't think of my reputation. I'm trying hard to be better than what I was. I want to be a better man. Hopefully, my behavior will bring a woman who will be right for me and the kind of future I'd like to have."

"What kind of future is that?"

He shrugged and became a bit bashful. "I've been thinking of settling down and having a family. I've run out of bitterness over what happened during my first marriage. I wanted happiness, love, kids, and most importantly, a real lady who wants the same and to grow old with me."

"Interesting."

He gave her a devilish grin. "Since we're killing time, share some of what turns you on."

She grinned with a hint of mischief. "I happen to think a man who is sensitive, confident, caring, and has a good sense of humor can be a turn-on."

"Does he have to have all the qualities you mentioned, or will he be accepted for one or two of them?"

"Are you making fun of me, Dr. Prince?"

"No, I'm only trying to understand you. All of that sounds good, but you haven't told me what gets you heated physically, you know, makes you a bad girl. A vixen."

"C'mon, I'm not telling you that." Sasha laughed nervously. She nodded toward the window. "The rain is letting up. We should be able to get to your car now."

Eric chuckled. "You wiggled your way out of that nicely. You got all your stuff? Let's make a dash for it." He studied the perfect profile of her face as he stood near her and was enticed by her pouty, sensual lips.

Since they'd been standing together and speaking of what turned each other on, Eric's blood had been humming with a brewing desire of the fantasies that danced in his mind. He'd tried his best not to imagine how it would be with her in bed, flesh to hot flesh, making torrid love.

"I'm all set and ready to make a dash for it."

Staring at her as though in a daze, he swept her into his arms and pulled her close to him and proceeded to kiss her in a heated manner.

Sasha, her blood rushing, and her heart racing at the out-of-the-blue action, surrendered to the passion of his kiss. As he maneuvered her against the wall, her arms went around his broad shoulders. His lips were warm, moist, and sweet. She loved the weight of his body pressing against hers; she couldn't resist arcing herself toward the strength of the man. Lost in a fog of intimacy, she wished this moment would never end.

Suddenly, the situation turned even more intense when she allowed him to slip his tongue inside her mouth. In the next instance, she felt his hand beneath her coat and on one of her breasts. He fondled it gently while delivering a deeper and hotter kiss. From the swirl of emotions he generated, her knees weakened.

She managed to end the session and pushed him away, trying to regain her composure. "Eric, wait. We can't do this. Not here." Her tone was breathy, and she touched his face, feeling the warmth from the passionate exchange. Pressing her back against the wall, she realized this virile man was the answer to all she wanted and needed.

Standing with his head lowered, Eric rubbed his lips as though they had been stung as he eyed her with lust. "Uh, I'm sorry the way I came on to you, but I sure don't regret it. In my arms you are everything I imagined you to be, and more."

Tentatively, Eric moved toward her and leaned close. He cupped her chin in his hand and tilted her face toward his for him to study. In the darkened building, the streetlight from outside the building illuminated them both. There was so much he wanted to say, but he was afraid to speak his mind. He knew he was going to have to slow things down a bit to win her trust further and to convince her he was no longer the player, and was ready for a real woman to share his heart, his soul, his all.

"You care for me. I felt your vibe, Sasha. Whether you want to admit it or not, you and I have something."

"We're physically attracted to each other. But I learned a long time ago that passion isn't enough to build a relationship on." Sasha remembered herself as a teen confusing sex for love and comfort during the most troubled time of her life.

"Oh, baby, there's no shame in passion between two consenting adults. This is all good," he said, his voice low and hypnotic. "We've got the sparks of something that we should continue."

"I can't be hurt or humiliated again."

"Believe me, I wouldn't do either of those. I know I have a bad rep to live down, but I've changed, Sasha. Give me a chance to show you how monogamous I can be. I'd like to date you for you to see that I'm more than a guy who loves 'em and leaves 'em." He laughed nervously. "There is even an explanation for that. I'm sure the bitterness of your divorce had you twisted to the point where you even did a few things you were ashamed of."

"Yeah, you've got me on that one. But I'm not making any confessions now. It's getting late, and I need to get home. My grandmother will be looking for that phone call from me to let her know I'm home and safe. She's a big worrier." Sasha fastened her coat and moved toward the door.

Eric took her hand and squeezed it gently. "Can we date?"

She offered him a smile. "If you and I did, can you imagine the gossip we'd create? People will be watching our every move."

"Forget them. It's about you and me."

"When we're working, you and I must maintain our professional relationship."

"If that's what you want, fine by me," Eric said, his voice filled with excitement.

"We can give it a try. Now will you please take me home? To my house."

"Hold up." He leaned toward her and delivered a slow and lingering kiss. "I'm serious about you, Sasha. My feelings are for real, and they aren't fleeting. I'm going to do whatever it takes for you to want to care for me the way I'm falling for you."

Hearing the sincerity in his voice and seeing it

on his face, Sasha offered him a hopeful smile. "I'm flattered . . . truly flattered. Day by day is easier for me to deal with. I have to admit, being kissed and held by you did feel nice and right." She held on tightly to his hand.

"In time you'll see that it's meant to be." He placed a tender kiss on her forehead and his arm around her shoulder as they left the clinic.

Settled into his car, Sasha dared to dream of a second chance at romance. Though the night was rainy and cold, her heart felt warm like sunshine, and her spirit was lifted as though it were spring, the season when all things reached out for life.

Chapter 6

After Eric had seen Sasha safely home, he picked up his cell phone to call his friend Miles. He wanted to get with him for some laughs and conversation, and his opinions. He flipped open his phone and saw he had several missed calls from Mia Evans. He grunted and didn't even consider returning her calls. He dialed Miles, who said he was at Dre's Bar and Grill. Eric told him he was on his way there.

When Eric made his way into the place, he was greeted by a couple of admirers with hugs and friendly kisses. He told the waitress to make sure the ladies had a round of drinks on him. This of course garnered more affection from the giggly women for him.

Reaching the table where Miles was entertaining a rather attractive woman, Eric hesitated. He didn't want to interrupt any game that Miles may have been laying on the lady.

"Miles, what's up, my man?"

"Eric, you made it. This young lady, Angelique, was keeping me company until you arrived. Angelique, this is my friend Eric Prince. Eric, this is Angelique Morris."

"Pleased to meet you." The young petite woman got up. "I'm going back to join my friends, Miles. Nice talking to you. I'll think about your offer." She sashayed away from the table.

Miles grinned at her sexy strut. "I can't stay out of trouble." He grunted. "I want it all, man."

"You'd better slow your roll, dude. You're still living with Rene." Eric removed his leather jacket and took a seat.

"That's done, man. We're going to separate," he said in a halfhearted manner.

"What? Is this what you really want?"

"I don't know. But one thing is certain. I'm not ready to get married, and Rene is. So that was the deal breaker for us."

"It's over for you two."

"It is." Miles sipped on his drink of vodka. "I'm not ready to talk about this anymore. Rene packed up and left. That was three days ago."

"Sounds to me as though you have regrets."

"Some. But I'm going to get through it. I intend to stay busy."

"From one brother to another, I don't think you should get out here with every woman who smiles at you. You aren't going to find the happiness you need."

"I can have a hell of a good time trying." Miles laughed loudly.

"Okay. I can see you getting caught up in a mess of drama."

Miles rubbed his fashionable bald head and grinned. "At least my life won't be boring. By the way, I've been wanting to talk with you to tell what else is going on with me."

"Another woman?"

Leaning forward, Miles said, "I've been out with your coworker friend's girl, Crystal Forbes. She is not shy and she knows how to make a man forget all of his problems." He settled back in his seat and chuckled.

"Are you into her? Or are you only using her?"

"Let's just say she and I are having fun for the present time."

"Women always say they are all right with the casual relationship, but in the long run they grow tired and want more. It never seems to fail, especially with the decent way Crystal came across to me."

Miles frowned at Eric as if he were a stranger. "Hold up. I know you aren't lecturing me on morals. Why are you trying to be sanctimonious all of a sudden? You were the one who taught me how to be a player."

"I did teach you some game, but that was when we were younger and when I was going through my divorce. Neither of us is getting any younger, and it's time for us to take life more seriously and start settling down. We've got to start being with women we can appreciate." Eric signaled for a waitress and ordered a sandwich and a beer.

"What's bringing all this bullshit out of you? Where is the freaky Eric who only wanted to score, make a conquest?"

"Man, I'm tired of juggling women, running game. It's getting tiresome. I wasn't raised to disrespect women the way I have been. I felt like being the bad boy was the only way I could get some of these women's attention. I believe some of our sisters are too hung up on drama. Some act as though it's an aphrodisiac for them. But I've got to be better, and so do you."

"I bet that nurse you introduced me to has you all twisted. Sasha Michaels is the one who is making you turn in your player's card." Miles laughed.

Eric smiled. "You've got me, man. She's for real. She's been through a lot in her life. If I want to get with her, I'm going to have to prove I'm a real man."

"From what I saw of her that night, I could see she was some kind of fine. I'd love to play doctor with her."

"Hands off, and keep your mind off her that way too. I'm going to make her mine."

As the waitress served them food and drinks,

Miles winked at the young woman and made her blush a rosy pink.

"There you go. Miles, if I were you, I'd reconsider my relationship with Rene. You and she have been together for three years. I don't blame the woman for wanting to get married. After all, she's a high school teacher. She's anxious to take her life to the next level with you. You used to be crazy about that woman. Surely, you haven't lost all those feelings you had for her."

Miles took a couple of sips of his beer. "I still care a lot about her, but marriage scares me, man. Not only is she talking about marriage, but she wants to have kids too. That's too much at one time. Then, to be really honest with you, I don't know if I have it in me to make a marriage work. I grew up in a houseful of women. I'm clueless as to what a husband is to do, and my old man left the family right after I was born."

"I'm sorry about all that. But your mother did a hell of a job raising you and your two sisters. I don't want to be the old man at the club, and I know you don't either."

"Look, I'm glad I'm mellow from the drinks I had before you got here. You've given me too much to think about."

"Good. I only have your best interest at heart. Rene is a good woman, and they are hard to find."

"True. But she is mad as hell at me for the way I was so willing to let everything we had fall apart.

But then there is Crystal, who is more than willing to comfort me through my troubled times."

"Rebound woman. You and she will have fun for a while, but you're going to find yourself thinking about Rene and what you two had and wishing you could get it back."

Miles smirked, then sipped on his drink. "Man, your old girl, Mia Evans, is here. She spotted us and is on her way." He chortled.

"Shit! Don't leave me alone with her. She's going to try to show out. I told her we were through the other night."

"Oh, damn! You are in for trouble. She's going to be a hard one to get rid of." Miles laughed under his breath.

Mia took a seat in their booth and sat close to Eric. She placed her hand on his knee and stared at him with her brown eyes, her pecan complexion dewy with perspiration.

"I figured you'd be here." She spoke loudly. "How come you haven't returned any of my calls? I've been trying to call you to see how you were. I care about you, and I thought we could still maintain a friendship and be civil, even if we aren't as close as I'd like us to be."

Her crude attitude turned Eric off, not to mention her breath reeked of alcohol and peppermint. He removed her hand from his leg. He wanted to get rid of her, but if he didn't do it in a tactful manner, she was going to get louder.

"You're here with me now. What is it that you have to say?"

With her glazed eyes, Mia stared at Eric as though he were speaking a foreign language.

Then she glanced at Miles as though she'd just realized he was there. "Hi, Miles," she said. "What am I going to do with this one? I've been good to him. I made him happy in every way a woman can. He doesn't want me around anymore. Can you believe that? He knows we're perfect and got that good, sweet chemistry together." She leaned across the table and took a sip of Miles's hard liquor. "He's got another woman. I'm not stupid. I'm gonna find out who she is, and I'm gonna tell her he has a woman. Me." In an attempt to hug Eric, she bumped the table and knocked over his beer, making a mess.

Eric jumped to his feet and wiped the front of his jeans.

"Oh, I'm sorry. I didn't mean to do that." She grabbed several napkins and began to wipe the front of his jeans, focusing on the zipper.

Eric snatched the napkins from her. "It's okay," he said in a controlled tone. "Miles, man, help me pick her up so I can take her back to the girlfriend I know she probably came with."

Miles took her by the arm and encouraged her to her feet. "Let me help you, baby."

"You are so kind. Look at Eric's pretty face. He's mad at me." Mia pulled away from Miles and fell on Eric, holding him around the waist and pressing her face to his chest. "Don't be mad. I love you. I still love you. I can't stop thinking about you." She began to sob loudly, making even more of a spectacle of herself.

"Let's go, Mia. You need to go home and get some rest," Eric said, trying not to sound harsh. He knew all eyes in the grill were on him. He hated the fact that she moved stubbornly in the high heels she was wearing. He slipped his arm around her waist and half dragged her toward the outside.

On the way, he spotted her girlfriend, who was busy talking with friends. He nodded for her to come get Mia. Once they were outside in the cool fall air, he released her and propped her up against the building.

He glanced back into the bar and wondered what was taking her friend so long. Suddenly, Mia was on him and looping her arms around his neck and trying to engage him in a kiss. She'd made contact with his lips, but he reared away from her.

She became boisterous. "How dare you push me away like I'm trash! You used to love everything about me. You were all over my body. You know you still want this." She leaped at him and began pounding him on the chest. "I hate you, Eric. I'm not going to let you get away with the way you walk all over my emotions. You're gonna pay."

Taking hold of her wrists to halt her blows, Eric noticed a small crowd was gathering. He was relieved when Cathy appeared and rushed over to her.

"Shut up, Mia!" Cathy said, tugging Mia and slipping her arm around her waist to hold her up. "You're making a fool of yourself. She's been drinking all evening and crying over you," she said to Eric.

"Do you want me to help you with her?"

"No, thanks. You've done enough," Cathy said.

Eric heard Mia sobbing and talking loudly, until he escaped from the scene back into the bar to find Miles.

He dropped down in his seat in the booth exhausted and humiliated. "Can you believe that?"

He ordered fresh drinks from the waitress. He remained silent and looked out the window. Filled with shame, he knew he had to take responsibility for what had occurred. He had used the woman and toyed with her emotions. Now she wanted what he couldn't give her. He realized more than ever that there was no such thing as casual sex. One paid a price for everything one did in the long run.

"Hey, don't let her faze you. I told you not to get involved with that one anyway. She had that vibe of having fatal attraction tendencies."

"I sure hope those threats of hers were only empty ones. I don't want any trouble in my life now that I'm trying to change and be a better man."

When the drink arrived, Eric gulped half of it down. "I hope she wakes up in the morning feeling like a fool after her girl tells her how she acted." He laughed nervously.

"For your sake, I hope Mia is done too. She had *crazy* written all over her for a while, though." He got up. "Excuse me. I'll be back. I got to check out this honey sitting at the bar. She's been eyeing me. Let me go fulfill the fantasy I see in her eyes."

"Man, you just won't learn. Getting with a woman you hardly know should be the last thing on your mind after what you just witnessed with me."

Miles grinned. "Man, I can look out for myself and keep my women in check. I'll catch up with you later."

"I'm leaving, man. I've had enough excitement for one evening." Eric paid his tab, slipped on his jacket, and got up and left.

Outside in the crisp air, rain began to fall again. Eric pulled the collar of his jacket up, thinking of the pleasant times he'd shared with Sasha earlier. Her sweets lips, her quiet spirit, and her beauty sparked a warm glow within him, erasing the bad experience in the grill.

Chapter 7

The Friday after Thanksgiving Day, Sasha was pleased to leave work and arrive home to an empty house. She had spent Thanksgiving Day at her grandmother's cooking and preparing dinner for a few friends and family members, and had eaten more than she should have of her grandmother's irresistible food. She'd invited Eric, but he had an invitation from friends of his family that he couldn't back out of. Her son, Craig, had ridden with his great-grandmother to Richmond for a few days to take some food and cheer to Sasha's grandmother's sister, who was sick and shut in.

Sasha turned on her sound system and tuned it to her favorite soul music station. Then she decided to take a long, leisurely bubble bath with bath salts she had bought months ago. After her bath, she planned to begin reading one of the many novels she had stacked in her to-be-read pile.

After luxuriating in her tub for nearly an hour, Sasha felt relaxed and ready for a nap. As she stepped out of the bath, her house phone rang. She rushed to answer it, thinking it was her grandmother, who had promised to call as soon as they'd arrived and gotten settled in at her great-aunt's.

"I was hoping I'd find you home," Eric said. "I overheard your conversation in the lounge today with Pam. So your son is out of town and you're all alone. Why didn't you tell me? You and I could have gotten together."

"Well, as I remember, you told me you had plans with some friends of yours. You sounded as though whatever was going on was a big occasion."

"There you go assuming. I'd rather spend time with you. I'm sure I'd find you more interesting."

"Would you like to come over, Eric?" she asked, with a hint of amusement.

"I thought you'd never ask."

Sasha laughed softly. "Give me about an hour, okay?"

"Sure enough. I'll see you then."

The moment Sasha hung up the phone, she hurried into a pair of gray leggings and a pink T-shirt with *Hope Hospital* on the front. Then she hurried into the living room to clear away the clutter of magazines and comic books left behind by her son.

Her next stop was the kitchen, where she had left behind breakfast dishes and the remains of the Chinese food she'd had for dinner. She took all the dishes and placed them in her dishwasher and emptied the trash can that Craig should have emptied.

After lighting scented candles in the living room, she turned on the television and tuned it to a crime drama.

Eric knocked on her door exactly an hour after she had hung up her phone.

"You've made it," she said warmly, opening the door for his entrance.

Eric, looking dashing in his brown leather jacket, blue pullover sweater, and jeans, greeted her with a slow smile. "The time couldn't get here fast enough," he said, strolling past her into the apartment.

"Let me have your jacket, to hang it up for you."

Freeing himself from the soft leather jacket, Eric revealed his athletic, fit body. As he handed his jacket to her, Sasha stared at him, desiring to touch him. "Have a seat. Make yourself comfortable." She turned away and went to the closet to hang up the coat.

Sasha couldn't ignore the scent of the expensive cologne on his coat. She returned to the living room and stood before him, her hands clasped. "How about some refreshments?"

"No, thanks. Come join me on the sofa, so we can talk." Eric thought Sasha looked like a sweet college coed in her outfit. He admired the way her snug T-shirt clung to her full breasts. Hints of her perky nipples revealed she was braless and sent his imagination to work. Her hair was pulled back into her familiar ponytail, and she wore gold hoop earrings, further enhancing her sex appeal.

Sasha took a seat beside Eric and folded her legs beneath her.

"Even though we've been out a couple of times, this is the first time I've actually been inside to see your apartment. I like it. It's you. It's cozy and all of your things reveal something of your interests." Eric crossed one long leg over the other and settled back, his arm stretched behind her.

"I'm glad you like it. I tried to make it as homey as possible for my son and me. I'm down-to-earth. One day when I can afford a home, I'd like to get a bit fancier with my interior decorating."

Eric nodded. A framed school picture of a young man on the coffee table caught his attention. "Is this your son?" Smiling, he reached for the picture and held it. "I can see you in him. He has your eyes and that great smile of yours. He's fourteen, huh?"

"My baby is growing up fast. He's as tall as I am now."

Eric put the picture back on the coffee table. He touched the photo album and looked to Sasha. "May I?"

"Of course." Sasha sat upright and a bit closer to Eric, to share the album with him.

The first few pages had early pictures of Craig in school and in their old neighborhood in northern Virginia in various activities at the recreational center there.

"He's looks like a great kid. I hope I get a chance to meet him soon."

"When the time is right, you will," she said without looking at Eric. Sasha hadn't introduced the two because she first wanted to see how well she was going to get along with him.

Eric continued to turn the pages and study younger pictures of her as a wife and a much younger mother. There were several pictures of her with Trey and toddler Craig in the park on a couple of rare occasions. The shots had been taken during a happy and idealistic time in their marriage, when they believed that love would see their marriage through anything.

"That's Trey, Craig's father, my ex-husband. I hold on to those for Craig's sake. They will be his when he's grown and leaves me to go on his own."

"I see."

Eric continued through the remainder of the book until he came across pictures of Sasha when she was about six years old, standing outside a school, holding the hand of a lovely woman, who was beaming. Sasha was adorable with her pigtails, backpack, and lunch box.

"This has to be the first day of school for you," Eric said, eyeing her and grinning. "Aren't you cute? Is that your mother?"

"Yeah, that's my mom. She went in late to work that day after seeing me off at school."

Eric noticed Sasha's eyes lost a bit of luster and filled with yearning. There were other pictures of a young Sasha and a few of her mother.

As Sasha got older, her mother's pictures showed less regard for her appearance, and she looked thinner and sadder, but always forced a look of happiness when she had her daughter by her side. Embarrassed by the changes her junkie mother had gone through, Sasha closed the book and returned it to the table without looking at Eric.

"I certainly could use some refreshment. I imagine you can too." She hopped up off the chair and headed for the kitchen.

Eric could see that Sasha still bore pain and wished there was something he could say or do to ease it. As a physician he understood that most family members who lost someone to drugs experienced shame, humiliation, helplessness, and heartache, but through it all, they still grieved the waste of a life cut short. He wanted to go to the kitchen and take her in his arms and comfort her, but he could see she had too much pride to admit she was still in pain.

Eric watched television quietly for nearly

fifteen minutes before Sasha returned from preparing a tray of drinks and snacks.

She smiled. "Did you mention something to me about growing up in the suburbs?"

Pam had informed her that the Prince family was one of the few prestigious black families in northern Virginia. His father ran one of the top legal firms in the D.C. area.

"I sure did. What's wrong with that?"

"Not a thing. Why are you so defensive?" She sat beside him and served him a drink.

"I'm not defensive. It's just that most black people I meet want to give me stuff because of my background. I attended private schools, played soccer, attended debutante balls and all that other stuff. In other words, a lot of people, especially guys, try to tell me I'm not black enough because I haven't come from the hood, that I don't know the struggle of blacks."

Grinning, Sasha shook her head. "Well, all black people are supposed to have the same experiences. We all have to be alike. Didn't you know that?"

He chuckled. "No. I missed those meetings."

"Good. Spoken like a real brother." Settling back on the chair, she said, "I bet it was great growing up and being you. You had a chance to be a real kid, unlike some of us. When you come from the inner city or a blue-collar family like I did, you have to grow up fast, and sometimes you find yourself looking for love in all the wrong places."

"Was that why you married so young, the situation with your mother?"

Lowering her head, Sasha responded softly, "My grandparents raised me when my mother couldn't, and then after she passed. They worked hard to take care of me and to cover their bills. My grandmother was a cook in the public school, and my grandfather took a job as a part-time janitor to supplement his Social Security. I was sort of left alone. I didn't let too many others in my life, besides Crystal. She was cool with me, but there were a lot of other kids who grew up with me, and in school, who made fun of me because of my mother's behavior. When you have a mother who is doing any and everything for a high, there is always plenty of fodder for jokes and cruel stabs at you when you're trying to rise above it all."

"Those days are gone. You survived it."

"True, but the words can be like stones. Some of it still haunts me, but I refuse to let it get me down."

Eric sat closer to her and placed his arm around her and squeezed her shoulder.

Resting her head on his shoulder, she said, "Tell me about your life. I'd like to know what it's like to grow in a 'Huxtable-like' environment."

"It's not all that. My mother and father were like any other parents. They made sure my sister and I stayed on the straight and narrow. You do know there is drama even in the suburbs. A lot of kids are spoiled and act out, doing stuff like any other kid who doesn't have supervision. The only difference is, lots of times the bratty ones will get sent to a therapist or away to boarding school with hopes of them straightening out their issues."

Feeling cozy at his side, she decided to ask him about his failed marriage.

"I married right out of college, thinking it would be one of those forever things. I thought I was set for one of those long-term marriages, like my parents. I was ready to have kids too. I believed I was going to have it all with the young woman I'd married. She and I had a boyfriend-girlfriend thing since we attended the same prep school, but once I got married, the sweet girl I knew didn't want any responsibilities. She insisted we hire a maid, so she could have her career. She and a few of her friends wanted to start a magazine like *Essence*. She was always away from home and making trips to New York to get a distributor or to network. When that dream didn't come through, she decided she wanted to become a screenwriter. She was consumed with it. She did hook up with a friend, and the two of them managed to launch a successful black comedy. So she ended up leaving me and moving to Los Angeles, where she could do her thing without anyone or anything to hold her down. She claimed me and the whole marriage weren't at all what she'd envisioned. She had too many dreams and goals to realize to be smothered by being my wife. That hurt. I was young and not as tough as I've become. But what hurt me worst was when I learned she had moved in with a well-known black film director and movie producer."

Eric removed his arm from around her shoulder and took her hand. "I've learned my life lesson from that, and I've moved on. It looks to me as though you're doing the same. You can't hold on to people who don't want to be in your life, right?"

"That's so true. When you're young it takes so long for you to realize when it's time to simply let go."

Eyeing her, Eric asked, "Have you let go of your bitterness?"

"I have. I only have to deal with my ex-husband for my son's sake. I don't bad-mouth Craig's father to him. I always try to be civil whenever Trey does visit or Craig has to speak to him."

"I don't have any dealings with my ex-wife. It's a done deal between the two of us."

Momentarily, the two remained silent as they watched the cable news channel. All the while, Eric held on to her hand.

"Let's see what else is on. I'm not feeling this depressing news." Sasha freed her hand and reached across Eric for the remote.

He placed his hand on the remote to keep it from her. "I didn't come to watch television. I came to be with you." He leaned toward her and placed a tender kiss on her lips, palming the side

of her face and pulling her toward him as he settled his back on the sofa. He was pleased when
he felt Sasha relax and relent to his affection. To
him, that moment felt so right and sweet. Enfolding her in his arms, he held her tightly.

Reeling from the strength of his embrace,
Sasha was at ease returning his tender kisses.
Taking a breather from his kiss, she gazed into
his amber eyes. "You're pretty good. Those lips
are tasty." She rested her face on his chest.

Eric placed his hand on the back of her neck,
encouraging her to turn her face upward. "There's
plenty more where that came from."

They sat on the sofa mastering the art of kissing.
First, tender kisses, then heated openmouthed
ones that made her body ache with desire.

As they lay in a reclining position, he hovered
over her and had placed his hand on one of her
breasts and fondled it, while he mesmerized her
with the sensual motions of his lips and tongue.
Sasha grew moist, and a tingling feeling made
her part her thighs. The smacking noises of their
kisses and the heavy breathing electrified her.
Clinging to him, she pushed her tongue as deep
as she could inside his mouth.

Eric then moved on top of her, fitting his body
with hers.

Feeling his firm, impressive arousal pressed
against her mound, she resented the fabric of
her clothes. Sasha couldn't resist swaying her

hips to satisfy the sensation brewing in her "passion flower."

Suddenly, his lips and his tongue left her mouth, and he licked her eyelids and returned to her mouth, tracing her lips with the tip of his tongue and reentering her mouth.

To Sasha it was a mind-blowing simulation of the sexual act. Boldly, he removed his hand from on top of her shirt and slipped it beneath the fabric to her breasts.

Sasha gasped. She closed her eyes and enjoyed the feel of her nipples being rolled between his forefinger and thumb and Eric moving back and forth upon her. In the heat of the foreplay, they clung and groped each other.

Sasha's mind turned foggy. She removed her shirt and offered up her breasts to Eric, who tasted them as though he were getting nectar from fruit. She grasped his shoulders and moaned softly with delight.

Sasha cursed silently when the house phone rang. She was in heaven with Eric and didn't want to return to reality. She reached for her shirt to cover herself, as though the party on the line could see her torrid actions.

"Oh, uh, let me up. I have to get that." She rolled on her side to get the portable phone on a nearby table. Standing on wobbly legs and drunk from passion, she staggered into the kitchen to speak with her grandmother.

"I thought you had forgotten me." Sasha laughed nervously, her voice husky with passion.

"You were 'sleep, weren't you, sweetie? I didn't mean to wake you. I bet you're going to get some much-needed rest, being on your own."

"Uh, yeah, I had drifted off a bit."

"I'm calling like I promised I would. Craig and I had a nice trip. I even got him to talk more than usual." She laughed softly. "Your great-aunt sends her regards too."

"How is she?"

"She's a lot better. I'm sure our company and all this food I brought will cheer her."

"Tell Auntie I send my love. When my schedule allows, I'll be down to see her."

"Craig wants to say a few words to you, dear."

Sasha glanced in the living room and saw a reclined Eric with his clothes disheveled. Touching her face, she felt it was fevered from all the steamy desire that had been pumping through her veins from his marvelous love antics. A shiver went through her, thinking that if the phone had not rung, they might have crossed the boundaries.

She was snapped out of her reverie by her son's voice.

"Hey, Mom. Guess what?"

"What, baby?"

"I talked to Dad." Craig's voice was full of excitement. "Grand told me to give him a call."

Sasha's grandmother had been urging her to

get Craig to call Trey even though Trey hadn't called in the last few months.

"Oh, really?"

"He wants me to come spend a few days with him when I'm out of school for Christmas. He wanted me to talk it over with you, you know, get your permission. Can I, Mom? He wants me to get to know the twins—my little brothers."

Sasha was a bit jealous that her son was so anxious to go with his father. Had he forgotten how Trey kept putting off his visits and cutting phone conversations because he had business to attend to? That was during the time he was wooing his soon-to-be wife and right after their marriage. Sasha was skeptical of Trey's interest. She didn't want him to be set up just to be let down. Craig may have forgiven the numerous birthdays Trey missed, the last-minute cancelation of promised trips that never failed to leave him feeling low and with a sour attitude, but Sasha didn't. She wanted to protect her son's heart.

"I can imagine you'll be glad to be with him, and your new family, but let's talk about this more when you return from your visit."

"You've got to let me go. Dad really wants to see me."

"That's all good," she said in her no-nonsense voice. "We'll talk when you get home, okay?"

"Okay," Craig moaned. "Mom, the coach said he's going to give me some playing time in next Saturday's game. Will you be able to come?"

"That's great, Craig. I'm going to make sure I have that day off. I'm going to have to get some pictures of my athlete. Maybe you can e-mail some to your dad. How would you like that?"

"That'll be hot. I can't wait until he sees my skills."

"Yeah, you're right. Good night, son. Have fun."

"Good night."

Sasha's mood had altered. Craig's news had cleared her mind of any further passion. Then again, it was a good thing she had gotten the call. She and Eric were headed to a level that she wasn't quite ready for emotionally. She certainly had no regrets for the intimacy they'd shared. The experience had shown her she was more than ready to open her cautious heart.

She straightened her shirt and smoothed the ends of her hair as she returned to the living room.

Eric noticed the smoldering look had faded from Sasha's brown eyes. He sat upright, swung his feet to the floor, and adjusted his clothes. He had gotten the message that there would be no more love play.

"My grandmother and Craig are all settled in Richmond." Sasha took a seat beside Eric and reached for one of the drinks that had turned watery from neglect. She drank slowly.

"That's good to know." Eric reached for the other drink. He gazed at her. "I better drink this to cool off, and I could use a cold shower as well."

He grinned and shook his head. He placed his hand on her knee and caressed it. "You had me going. I hope you have no regrets. It was great while it lasted."

"Hmm. No. I had as much fun as you did. We came close to doing something we may have had second thoughts about, though."

"Not me. I'm ready, but I want you to feel comfortable if we should ever . . ."

"You are such a gent. I like that." Sasha leaned over to him and kissed him on the lips to show her appreciation for him understanding her and the slow route she had chosen to take.

Cupping her chin, he drew out that kiss as long as he could.

Sasha pulled away. "Phew! Let's leave things as they are for the evening."

"I'm cool. I'm settling for a little snuggling and sweet, innocent kisses for now."

Sasha laughed and snuggled beside him on the sofa. He placed his arm around her shoulder while they watched television.

It was nearly 1:00 a.m. when Eric was all set to leave, standing at the door in his jacket.

Sasha stood close to him and shared admiring stares. He kissed her tenderly, and she accepted it with pleasure.

Eric smiled. "Would you consider attending a wedding with me?"

"Whose wedding?"

"My sister, Ashley, is getting married the first

week in December. I'm a part of the wedding party. It's going to be a fancy affair. Fairy tale." He chuckled. "Come with me and keep me company. That way I can keep my family and friends at bay. I won't have to worry about anyone playing matchmaker."

Sasha was amused. "You want me to assume the role of your girlfriend? That's dishonest."

"Well, you are a girl and a friend for now. That's not really a lie. And I certainly have my hopes that this understanding we have will elevate to that level as soon as you can see that I'm the one for you." He tweaked her nose playfully.

Sasha grinned. "I love your persistence."

"I'm relentless. How about it?"

Sasha thought for a moment.

"C'mon, Sasha. Look at it as a minivacation. You'll have a chance to meet my family and friends and see the area where I grew up. I'll pay for all your expenses."

"I might take you up on that. It sounds very interesting. I like to see a fancy wedding too. They can be romantic."

"I've been there and done that. My wedding was all that flash and dash, but it didn't guarantee happiness. The next time I do it, it will be simple, small, beautiful, and it's definitely going to have no option for divorce." He chuckled.

Eric's description fit Sasha's idea of what she wanted for herself should she decide to make such a commitment again.

"Time for me to say good night." He kissed her on the forehead. "I probably won't sleep tonight, thinking of what could have been."

"Good night, Eric," Sasha said sweetly, opening the door.

He winked at her and vanished.

After closing the door, she leaned against it and sighed. Her body hummed from the pent-up passion she'd denied herself. Should there be another session like the one this evening, she felt as though she wouldn't be able to restrain herself.

Chapter 8

Since Dr. Prince had ended his relationship with Mia Evans, she had used way too many of her personal leave days at Hope Hospital to stay at home and feel sorry for herself. She'd had him in the palm of her hands. The relationship the two of them had was going great or so she thought. Mia had begun their friends-with-benefits thing with the idea that sex was sufficient between the two of them. He'd told her up front that he wanted no romance or commitment. He had been hurt and wanted nothing to do with love or romance. She agreed with his terms, having had her share of bad relationships too. In her thirty years of life, men had made promises, then broke them, leaving her high and dry. Even her father.

Eric Prince had been so gorgeous and charming that she took a risk on him, thinking he would appreciate a real sensual and uninhibited woman like her. Just maybe he would fall in love with her and give her the life she'd always dreamed of. She and Eric could have been a powerful couple together. Dr. and Mrs. Eric Prince could have been a part of Huntersville upper-crust social circle.

She had gone into the relationship for the sex, but she got caught up, and her emotions blossomed into love. Every time they were together, she found she was giving up a part of her spirit to him. She wanted him to be hers exclusively. And in moments of intimacy, she was hoping he would feel the vibe of her love, and see the intensity of passion on her face.

In the cafeteria of the hospital, she sat alone, trying to finish a bowl of soup. Her appetite hadn't been up to par. During the last few days she took off, she had lain around in her pajamas as though she were grieving someone's death. She had cried until she couldn't cry anymore.

"Lady, where have you been?" Pam asked.

"I've been out sick. I had some kind of bug," Mia lied, forcing a smile. She couldn't admit to Pam that she'd been suffering with a broken heart. Pam would spread the word, and everyone would know that Dr. Prince had dumped her. Everyone who resented her ambitious attitude would love hearing news like that.

Suddenly, Sasha and Dr. Prince strolled into the cafeteria and got into the serving line. Sitting straight up in her seat, Mia tuned out whatever Pam was saying and eyed the two of them.

She noticed a glow on Eric's face as he chatted with Sasha, who appeared to be extremely happy. Laughter came easy to both of them. Then she saw them staring into each other's eyes. Her heart sank when she realized that there was a mutual admiration between the two. He had never smiled at her like that or even bothered to look at her face with the kind of affection he lavished on Sasha Michaels. Deep in her heart, she was screaming. How dare he leave her for Sasha? She had gone to high school with Sasha, who was a loner and a bit of an outsider then. But she would have been too, if her mother was a junkie/tramp.

"Mia, are you all right? You look as though you're not feeling good." Pam stared at her with interest.

"I'm all right. This is my first day back. I still don't feel like myself, but I'm getting there." She laughed nervously. "Hey, what's up with those two?"

Pam looked over her shoulder eagerly. "Who are you talking about?"

"Dr. Prince. Look at the way he and Sasha Michaels are acting like a couple of teenagers."

Pam kept silent but wore a suspicious grin. She unwrapped her sandwich and was getting ready to take a bite.

"You know something," Mia told her, trying to hide her anxiousness.

"I don't know a thing."

Mia eyed them again. Eric paid for Sasha's

lunch and then directed the way to an empty table. Once they were seated, they continued to laugh and give each other lingering looks. So Sasha had taken her place. How dare he take Sasha over her. She had such a messed-up life.

Mia remembered the gossip when Sasha had gotten knocked up in high school and how she had gotten married in her teens. She remembered that good-looking Trey, who had just started college, was her baby's father. People in town used to talk of the disappointment of Trey's parents, who felt as though the responsibility of being a father and a husband so soon would keep their son from achieving his ambition of becoming a doctor. And they didn't want a girl with a shoddy background like Sasha to marry their son. No one could keep the young couple apart at the time.

"Mia, you know we've got a sorority meeting coming up soon. Are you planning on getting active again?"

"Huh? What?" Mia frowned at Pam.

Scowling, Pam looked to be taken aback.

Mia laughed nervously. "I'm sorry. My nerves are a bit jagged." Then she went on to discuss the sorority stuff with Pam, all the while keeping tabs on Eric and Sasha.

While Pam blabbed on, Mia's mind was on revenge. She wasn't going to allow Eric to dump her as coldly as he had. He owed her for all the time she had devoted to him. Damn, she wanted him back in her arms and in her bed. She was going to have to find a way to make it happen. She had to let him know Sasha wasn't for him.

Sasha had told Craig she had invited Eric to his first basketball game for Owens Middle School. Until now, she hadn't introduced the two. But the more she saw Eric, the more she liked him. This basketball game was an ideal setting for their first meeting.

By the time Eric strolled into the gym, the game had already begun.

Sasha noticed several other women in the crowd ogling him as he made his way toward her looking handsomely dressed in jeans and a burgundy sweater that emphasized his sex appeal. When he spotted her, their eyes locked. It pleased her how he gave her that charming smile of his that made her heart feel as though it were full of sunshine.

Reaching her on the bleachers, Eric asked, "Has he played yet?"

"Not yet, but he should be getting his time soon."

As Eric sat close to her, she felt a calmness.

"Hey, I believe I recognize him from the pictures you've shown me. He's number twenty-six, right?"

"Good. That's my boy!"

When the coach called Craig from the sideline,

Sasha jumped to her feet and clapped. She yelled above the noise, "Craig! Get 'em, Craig!"

Her son glanced in her direction, squinting. Then he grinned bashfully.

"My baby is going to do it. Yes, he is."

Sasha's pride and confidence for her son amused Eric. It was obvious that her son was her heart. He liked the spirit she exhibited. In his family, his parents were reserved and didn't exhibit affection the way she did. He took hold of her hand, and she gripped his hand while she focused on the floor action.

When Craig hustled to the basket against the aggressive rival for his two-point shot, Sasha gasped and leaned on Eric's shoulder. The shot went through the hoop. Sasha leaped to her feet, dragging Eric with her.

Embracing her and shouting with as much joy, Eric seemed thrilled for Sasha.

Craig was doing a fantastic job, until he was cornered and was unable to break through for another shot at the hoop. Making his way back down the court, Craig attempted to block the player from the opposite team, but the other boy wasn't having it and knocked Craig flat on his butt.

Gasping at the sight, Sasha jumped to her feet.

"He's okay. It's no big deal, baby."

Sasha was relieved when she saw Craig get to his feet and use the back of his arm to wipe his brow. She took her seat, infuriated by the treatment her son had received. "That was uncalled for. Why do they have to be so mean?"

Eric placed his arm around her shoulder. "It's part of the sport. Relax. He's doing fine." He placed a kiss on her face, to soothe her.

At the feel of his lips, Sasha's complexion turned rosy. "Eric, not here. Suppose Craig sees you."

"It's time he knows. He's going to be cool, I bet. I can't wait to meet him. After the game, I'd like for us to go for a bite to eat." Eric returned his focus to the court.

Although Sasha really liked Eric a lot, she hadn't said that much to Craig about him. She wanted to see if Eric was as interested in her as he seemed before letting Craig know him.

All of a sudden, a melee broke out on the court. Craig and a boy from the other team got into a shoving match that turned into a fight among the two teams. The coaches and the school security hurried and cleared the matter up to restart the game. However, Craig was sent to the bench, along with the rival player.

A disappointed Sasha couldn't take her eyes off her sulking and angry son's face. "I've never seen Craig act this way. What's with all this fighting?"

"He's a teenage boy who is standing up for himself. He doesn't want to be called a punk. It's a man thing."

"He's a boy, though."

"He's a boy who is growing into a man."

Sasha didn't like this side of Craig. She was

going to have to talk to him and make sure his anger only came out during sports.

By the time the final horn sounded, Craig's school had lost the game by three points.

Sasha and Eric waited in the gym for Craig. When he finally appeared, he looked disappointed and angry.

Sasha walked up to him and hooked her arm with his. "Don't look that way. That was only the second game of the season, right? It was a good game, and you played a great game." She smiled. "For a minute, though, I didn't know whether I had come to a street fight or a basketball game."

Craig shrugged. "It was messed up, Mom. We would have won that game if I hadn't been put out because of my foul."

"The next game you'll be able to shine more. You guys take this serious, so you're bound to win the next one. Maybe you fellows need to stop posing like the pro players and focus on your game."

"Aw, Mom, it's not that bad." Craig gave a curious stare at Eric, who stood beside Sasha.

Noticing his look, Sasha said, "Craig, this is a friend of mine—Dr. Prince. He's a physician at Hope Hospital. I also work with him at the Free Clinic. He came to keep me company and to see your game." She grinned. "This is my son, Craig. Craig, Dr. Prince."

Extending his balled fist for a pound, Dr.

Prince said, "Nice to meet you, man. You've got skills, and you sure didn't let them run over you."

Reluctantly, Craig pounded him in return. With an expressionless face, he turned to his mother. "I'm starved. Can we stop and get something to eat?"

"We sure can," Eric responded. "I'd like for us to go to Pizza Hut and pig out." He laughed.

"Whatever," Craig said in a dry tone. "Can we do it now?" He looked to his mother for an answer.

Her son's rudeness didn't please her. She gave Eric an apologetic look, and he returned it with an understanding one.

"How about we follow you to the restaurant?" Sasha suggested.

"Okay, that'll work."

Once that was settled, Craig marched away from them and burst through the gym's exit.

Sasha sighed. "Excuse his behavior. I'm sure he's bent out of shape over his game."

As they left, Eric draped his arm around her shoulder. "No apology is needed. He's an ordinary kid bursting with a mixed bag of emotions. I'm sure his disposition will change, once he loads up on some food."

"I certainly hope so."

During their visit to the Pizza Hut, Sasha was dismayed that Craig didn't engage in the interesting conversations that Eric and she tried to bait him into. He plowed through nearly a whole pizza and a couple of refills of sodas with little more than a simple yes or no answer to their questions.

"Sasha, are you still interested in catching that movie with me this evening? I'm off duty for the rest of the day, so we won't be disturbed."

Craig glanced at his mother and waited for her response.

"Since this is the first Saturday I've had off in a while, I'd love to see it. There's been so much positive buzz about this new Will Smith movie, I'm looking forward to checking it out. How about an eight o'clock showing? I have to go home and catch up on my laundry and a few other household chores." Sasha noticed Craig's interest in her conversation with Eric.

"Mom, I want to see it too. May I go with you guys?"

"What do you say, Eric?" Sasha gave Eric a victorious look.

Eric stared at Craig. "You're perfectly welcome, my man."

Although he'd been looking forward to an evening alone with Sasha, Eric was willing to let the kid come along, to win him over. Also, he sensed that Craig figured that there was more than friendship between him and his mother. Eric saw the green-eyed looks Craig gave him whenever he touched Sasha's hand or placed his arm around her shoulder.

* * *

That evening when the three of them went to the movie, Craig was in a much better mood. He left Sasha and Eric alone when he saw a couple of his teammates. He chose to sit with his boys a couple of rows behind her and Eric.

After the movie, Craig didn't hesitate to fall into a conversation with Eric over the action film. He even brought up other action movies he loved and was surprised to learn that Eric had enjoyed them as much as he had. Eric owned a couple of other flicks that Craig hadn't seen, and he promised to loan them to Craig for his viewing.

The moment they arrived home from the movies, Sasha told her son to take his key and to go on into the house. Craig wasted no time leaving the couple. Taking off, he mumbled something about being able to catch a classic game on the ESPN channel.

Since the night wasn't too cold, Eric encouraged Sasha to stand outside to talk a bit. He leaned against his car and pulled her to him.

"Have you spoken to him about us yet?"

"No, I haven't. I decided to wait until after we went to the movies. I figured a second chance for you to be with him today would make him more acceptable to you, and I believe it has."

"He was more open, and friendlier too."

As Eric gazed upon Sasha's face, he pushed back a piece of hair that kept blowing in her face.

Brushing it back in place, he kissed her tenderly. "He's going to put it all together. He's a sharp kid. You can tell him, or he'll figure it out on his own."

"I'll talk to him. Soon."

"Good. It'll be for the best." He held her tighter. "Every time I see you or am with you, I want you more. I've given up all other women for you. I'm not the same man, Sasha. In fact, now that I've held you and kissed you, gotten to know you, I don't ever want to be the bitter man I was."

Hearing the sincerity in his voice and being held against his strong body, Sasha couldn't deny that she had fallen for Eric Prince.

"Yes, you have changed. I've noticed you're calmer and not as intense. I've never had a man go through so many changes for me." She wrapped her arms around his neck and rested her forehead against his cold nose. "Come in for a while. I can fix us some hot chocolate to warm us."

Without saying a word, he gave her a lingering kiss that sent heat through her veins. He sighed. "I'm heated now, but I'm still coming in for your hot chocolate."

When they entered the house, Craig was slumped on the sofa, watching television.

Eric made an attempt at conversation, but Craig didn't have much to say. Sasha and Eric exchanged knowing looks. Eric stayed long enough to drink a cup of hot chocolate and to chat with Sasha. Then he decided to call it a night.

At her front door, he kissed her briefly.

"It looks as though we're back to square one."
He chuckled.

"Don't worry. I'll talk to him."

"I'll call you later, baby."

Sasha nodded and closed the door as Eric disappeared outside to the parking lot. Whirling away from the door, she met Craig's inquisitive stare.

"Mom, you like that dude, don't you?"

Sasha moved across the room and took a seat. She began straightening the clutter of magazines there. "Uh, I do like Eric." She returned her son's intense look.

"When I peeked out the window to see what was taking you so long to come in, I saw y'all kissing and hugging. In the movies, he kept his arm around you like you were his girlfriend or something."

Staring at him, Sasha was amused. He made her feel as though he was the parent and she was the virginal daughter he was trying to protect from the bad boy.

"So, he's your boyfriend."

"In a way, son. We've only been seeing each other for a little while."

The response didn't excite Craig. He continued staring at the television as though he hadn't heard her.

"Don't you like Eric—Dr. Prince? You and he seem to have a few things in common."

"If you marry that dude, do you expect me to call him *Dad*?"

"You have only one father. There's no need for us to talk about marriage. Eric and I have to know each other longer before we make a serious commitment like that."

Her son made no comment, his teenage expression unreadable as a stone.

"Uh, I've been meaning to tell you, while you're gone to visit your father next weekend, I've decided to attend Dr. Prince's sister's wedding that is being held out of town. I'll be gone for the same amount of time as you." She smiled.

"For real?"

"Yes, Eric wants me to meet his family and to sort of be his date."

"No doubt he is your man, Mom."

"Excuse me, young man?"

Grinning mischievously, Craig said, "I'm not trying to be disrespectful, but you wouldn't be going through all these changes if he didn't mean anything to you."

Realizing her son was maturing, she couldn't do anything but smile.

Craig returned his attention to his program as though the whole thing wasn't a big deal.

When her house phone rang, she checked the caller ID and was pleased it was Eric. "Yes," she answered in a sultry tone and floated to her room for privacy.

"I couldn't wait to get home to call you. I had to hear that sweet voice of yours. And I was also concerned about Craig. It looks as though I'm going to have to toe the mark to win him over. I can understand the feelings he has at his age. He's probably afraid of losing your affection and attention."

She laughed softly. "Craig has gotten you nervous. I've spoken to him and I told him you and I care for each other. He had nothing to say. Let's give him a few days to get used to the idea. I have a feeling he'll be fine. The key is, I have to make sure he feels that nothing will change between me and him as mother and son."

"That sounds reasonable enough. From what I see, you and he have a good relationship. You've done a great job of raising him."

"Thanks. Mothers like to hear compliments like that. You're due a gold star for what you said."

"Lucky me. I hope to get plenty of those. Your happiness is definitely my priority."

Laughing softly and with delight, she continued. "I did tell Craig I would be going out of town for the wedding with you. That's going to work out perfectly. It happens to fall on the same weekend he is to go to his father's house out of town."

"Everything is all set, huh? Is Craig still up?"

"He is. In fact, I wouldn't be surprised if he's standing in the hallway trying to hear what I'm talking about. He can be nosy."

Eric chuckled. "Call me when he's knocked out for the night. I want to talk longer."

"Will do."

After the call, Sasha went to the kitchen and

decided to heat her kettle for a soothing cup of tea. She wanted to take a few moments for herself to think over the wonderful day and everything she had come to like about Eric.

"Okay, Craig, it's your bedtime. You've had a long day. Move it."

"I'm going, I'm going."

Then she heard him stomp off to his room and close his bedroom door.

Alone in the kitchen, she turned on the small television on the counter and turned to a late-night talk show. Her mind wasn't on the program. It was on the trip, attending the fancy wedding and meeting Eric's family. *What better way to get to know a man than to meet his family and friends?* she mused.

Chapter 9

The Thursday before his sister's wedding, Eric had been working long hours at his ob/gyn practice. There had been an outbreak of a flulike virus and cold symptoms for his mothers-to-be that required his medical attention to make sure that the women would take care of themselves for their babies' sakes. He had instructed his receptionist to work in any patients who called and complained of feeling ill. The only things that kept him from feeling overwhelmed were his thoughts of the big weekend with Sasha and his family.

Around three o'clock that afternoon, Dr. Prince picked up the chart from the front door of one of his exam rooms and couldn't believe the name of the patient who waited inside for him. Seeing the name Mia Evans, he hoped it was just another woman with the same name of the woman he wanted no further dealings with.

Before entering the exam room, he took a deep

breath and made a wish that it wasn't her. He wasn't in the mood for any irrational behavior.

As Mia sat on the end of the exam table, her glossy lips formed a shy smile. "Dr. Prince, how are you?"

"I was fine. You know this isn't a good idea. I'm sure you have another doctor you can see."

"I'm overdue for a pelvic exam. I thought I'd come to the best doctor in town—*Dr. Feelgood.*"

"I don't have time for games, Mia. I hate to think what lie you told my receptionist to get an appointment. You aren't pregnant and look physically healthy."

"I—I want you—as my gyn. After all, you have the best reputation in town for keeping your ladies satisfied and happy. Also, I'm proud to say from experience, you know a woman's body and exactly how to touch it. Stroke it."

"That's it. I don't believe you really need an exam today. I'm going to give you the name of a colleague who will give you an appointment for another time."

"I bet you wouldn't treat Sasha Michaels as mean as you're treating me."

He shot her an evil look, but said nothing.

"The secret is out. I've seen you with her. She's the one you want now. I sure hope you don't break her heart the way you did mine. You made me love you, and then you detached yourself without any warning." Her brown face held a tortured expression. "I can't understand why you want her. Surely, you don't know about her. Her past."

"I don't want to hear anything from you. I'm

sure whatever you say is going to be a lie. Stay out of my life."

Mia hopped off the table and walked toward him, a hand on her hip and a vengeful look in her eyes. "Sasha Michaels is probably as trampy as her mother was. I bet she didn't tell you how she shamed her family by getting pregnant when she was still in high school. Did she tell you her mother was a crack whore who would do anything for money to get high? I know she has you fooled with all those sophisticated airs she puts on and with her nursing degree. She couldn't hold on to her husband. He only married her because he had to, and he probably lived in fear of her turning out to be as pathetic as her mother was."

"That's enough, Mia. I won't listen to any more of your vileness. And I certainly won't listen to you speak of Sasha that way." He snatched the chart and headed for the door.

Mia lunged for the door before he could open it and threw herself against it, blocking his path. Taking hold of the lapels of his white med jacket, she said, "I'm hurting, Eric. When we started hooking up, we agreed there would be no love involved. I broke the rules. My emotions got entangled with what we did between the sheets. I'm miserable without you. Can't we go back to what we had? I don't want to feel as though I was only a means of relieving sexual tension for you. Give us more time. I will make you love me."

Eric hated being drawn into this mess. The desperation in her eyes and voice was frightening.

He still had a roomful of patients. He certainly didn't want to create a scene that would show him in a bad light. He knew he was going to have to come up with a way to get her out of the office without any obvious drama.

In a feigned comforting manner, he took hold of her shoulders. "Pull yourself together. You're obsessing over this unnecessarily. It's over, Mia. I'm not going to make any deals with you. I'm not the same man who slept with you. It's time for us both to move on."

Closing her eyes, Mia said, "I don't know if I can. I was hurt badly before I found you to ease the humiliation I'd endured. You made me feel like a real woman, Eric." Opening her tearful eyes, she gazed at him. "I was in a live-in relationship before you. I had hopes of getting married to the man. Then one day I came home early from work to find my man . . . my man in bed with another one. It was an utter nightmare to me." Mia's voice quivered, and her eyes revealed the humiliation she spoke of.

In all the times they'd been together, Mia had never gone into details about this incident, the same way he hadn't spoken of the pain he'd suffered from his broken marriage.

Whenever Mia showed up after he called for her, the two of them would have enough drinks to numb their emotional bruises and then hit the bed. In the morning, Eric always remembered feeling as empty and lonely as ever.

Sasha's quiet personality and ladylike sophistication had cleared away the darkness for him, and his need to use alcohol and sex to ease his mind and heal his heart.

Suddenly, Mia took hold of his face and gave him a hard and awkward kiss.

He gripped her wrists and glared at her. "This has to stop."

Weeping, she said, "How can you not want me? Love me?" She quivered. "You were supposed to fall in love with me. I was going to be Mrs. Prince and make you the happiest man alive." Her face was a mask of confusion and sadness.

"I'm going to give you something to relax you. Then I'm going to call your roommate, Cathy, to come get you and take you home to rest. Does that sound good?"

She nodded her head as she pulled away from him, her face smeared with tears. She slid to the floor and sat. Then she pulled her knees up to her chest and buried her face in her folded arms.

Immediately, Eric went to the phone and called his nurse for assistance. The nurse arrived quickly.

"This young woman has emotional problems," he explained. "I'm going to give her an injection of ten milligrams of Valium." He went to his cabinet and prepared the injection and administered it in Mia's arm. Then he scribbled Cathy's number on a piece of paper. "This is Miss Evans's roommate's cell number. Call her and have her come here to pick her up. I'm going to let Miss Evans rest in here until her ride comes. When her ride comes, send for me. I'll give her the name of a therapist who can administer the help she needs. I'll stay with her until you've done that." Eric sighed with remorse and regret at the sight of Mia, who now rested on the table.

Mia lifted herself on her elbows. She looked dazed. "You and I will be together again. Sasha won't be around forever. I'll be waiting for you. I'm going to make you want me. You love me as much as I love you. I know this." She fell back on the exam table and began to giggle as though what she'd said would actually become a reality.

When Eric's nurse returned to let him know she had contacted Mia's roommate and that she was on her way, he instructed the nurse to stay with Mia. Eager for a moment of silence, he fled the exam room for his office. He plopped into his leather chair behind his desk and closed his eyes. If only he could turn back the hands of time and avoid falling into the sexual games he had played. He prayed that Mia was done with all this madness and would be able to move on with her life, so he could do the same with his. He had found his chance at real happiness and wanted nothing or no one to keep him from it.

The Friday that was to begin the big weekend, Trey Michaels sat in Sasha's apartment with a haughty attitude. She had spoken to him several times on the phone, but she hadn't seen him since packing up and moving from northern Virginia more than six months ago. Being alone with him while Craig did his last-minute packing, she was pleased to realize she had no feelings at all for this man anymore. The anger, the impatience, and the inferiority that often dogged her in his presence no longer affected her. At last, she could say she was free of all the emotional baggage from their failed marriage, and was truly ready to move forward with her life.

"Trey, tell me, how is your family?"

"They're all doing great. Thanks for asking. The babies are growing up so fast. We just got new pictures returned of them the other day, and they are something else."

His smile reminded her of Craig's. "I bet you have some to show off." Sasha couldn't remember Trey being so enthusiastic over Craig's early pictures.

Looking surprised yet pleased by her request, Trey dug out his wallet and opened it to the picture he was most proud of. "My six-month-old sons."

Sasha took the wallet. She was pleased to see Craig's recent school picture on the other side of the twins. Sasha couldn't help but admit they were adorable. "So that's Trey and Ray. Their picture reminds me of how Craig looked at that age. Don't you think?"

"I'll say. They're a lot like Craig, but a double of everything about him." He chuckled.

"I'm sure Craig is going to love being with them. He has brothers who will make him feel more mannish than he tries to act now."

As Trey put the pictures away, he noticed

her red suitcase standing in the corner with Craig's things.

"You've got an outing planned too, huh?"

"I'm going away to a wedding with a friend."

"Good. Have fun." He rubbed his hands together. "Uh, Sasha, I've apologized to Craig over the phone for not keeping in touch with him the way I should have. I've been so busy with my practice, and my wife had a difficult pregnancy that required me to spend extra time with her. For a while, it was one thing after another. I didn't worry about Craig, because I knew he was in good hands with you and your grandmother. And, my goodness, he is far from a baby. I can't believe how much he's grown since the last time I saw him. There's not much fathering left for me to do, is there?"

"I wish I could agree, but he's at the age where he is going to need you more than ever. While he's with you, take time to really talk with him. I have a feeling he has conversations for you that he would feel embarrassed having with me."

Sitting back in his seat, Trey looked worried. "I got you. I'm going to see what's on his mind." He looked as though he took offense to Sasha reminding him of his duty as a father.

"Better late than never. By the way, I didn't mention to you that he's been having problems with anger in school. Also, he's been showing a lot of interest in these fast girls at his school. They are after him. They call the house, and one or two have even shown up at the house. Lately, I've been making him go to my grandmother's after school to keep him from any temptations. I've given him my side on the boy-girl relationship, but it would be good for you to wise him up even more. We certainly don't want him to repeat the same mistake we did when were young and starry-eyed."

Sasha noticed Trey's face turning somber. The polite moments were over. She braced herself for the verbal eruption.

"You got that right." Trey smirked. "I'm going to educate him as much as I can. I'll be sure to tell him that just because he has sexual desires for one woman, it doesn't necessarily mean that he's in love. I'm going to show him about condoms and how to protect himself when he's older. I clearly don't want him living a life of undue stress, frustrations, regrets that come from being burdened with a family before he's had a chance to enjoy being a man himself."

Insulted by his minilecture, Sasha glared at Trey. Even though she had stopped loving him, she still treasured their young romance and the early years of their marriage. She had no clue he had viewed their young marriage so negatively. Of course, there was bitterness, but Trey had never said it aloud the way he had just done.

Not wanting to get caught up in a war of words, Sasha marched off to Craig's room to hurry him along. She returned to the living room with Craig, who had an overstuffed backpack to go along with his other piece of luggage.

"I'm all set, Dad." Craig tossed his junk on the sofa and slipped into his overcoat.

Sasha stood with her arms folded and watched her son. She could feel Trey, eyeing her, but she was so vexed by him, she wouldn't look at him.

Raising from his seat, Trey said, "Let's get on the road, son. Give your mom a hug." He picked up Craig's backpack.

Rushing up to Sasha, Craig hugged her. "See you later."

"You behave yourself. Don't be too rough with the babies, son."

Trey gave Sasha an apologetic look. "He's going to be fine, Sasha. Uh, you've done a wonderful job with him. Together we'll clear up these growing issues he's going through."

Sasha smiled politely.

Watching Craig dash out the door, Trey hesitated. "I'm sorry for what I said. I'm stressed. The last few days have been extremely busy for me." He stared at her with warmth. "Despite the bad times we had, I still remember the good too. We did our best. It just wasn't meant to be."

"Whatever, Trey. Take care of him, and I'll see you guys on Sunday evening."

"Have fun, Sasha. You look like you could use a trip."

"Gee, thanks. Bye," she said, closing the door.

Chapter 10

Eric arrived at Sasha's an hour after Trey had left with Craig. The moment she opened the door, Eric lavished her with his wonderful smile.

"Are you all packed and ready for our adventure?"

"I sure am." She slipped into her short jacket and grabbed her purse. Then she pointed to the red luggage for him to carry. "I can't wait to meet your family."

"They're looking forward to meeting you too," he said as they left her apartment for his car. "We've got to get on the road. There's going to be a rehearsal at five o'clock in the church chapel. I hope the traffic is steady for us. You know my mom and sister have already assigned me chores to take care of the moment I get there."

"Since it looks as though you're going to have a full evening, I was thinking I should stay at the hotel tonight and rest. I don't want to be in the way. I can imagine everyone is more than on edge at this point. Tomorrow I feel will give me a better chance to meet everyone after the big wedding ceremony."

"Are you sure? You wouldn't be in the way."

"I think it'll be for the best.

"Okay. Tomorrow you can join the family back at the house as well, and all of us are planning to attend church on Sunday," Eric informed her as he drove away from her neighborhood and headed for the interstate.

"If you like, you come visit me in my room once you're done with all your family duties this evening." Sasha reached over and touched him on his knee.

A smile eased from the corners of his mouth. "Your sexy factor just went up five points. I'm getting to you, huh? I don't know how I'm going to focus on anything, knowing you're waiting to be with me at the end of all this wedding foolishness."

The drive from Huntersville to Springfield was wonderful. Sasha and Eric listened to great music and had engaging conversation and generous laughs involving subjects they hadn't discussed before. With a good flow of traffic and having each other's company, the traveling time went by quickly. Soon Eric was pulling up in front of the Marriott Hotel and assisting Sasha up to her room.

Once they'd gotten settled inside her room,

Eric's cell phone began to buzz. He informed her it was Ashley.

As Sasha set to unpacking, Eric had fallen upon her double bed to rest. He placed a hand behind his head and eyed Sasha admiringly.

"Okay, sis. I'm going to have time to do that and more. Chill out. All you need to do is focus on your man and doing whatever you have left to do to get down the aisle. Mom and Dad have gotten you one of the best wedding planners they could find, so you wouldn't have to stress. Have a glass of wine and pull it together. I'll be at the house shortly."

Eric hung up his cell and sat up on the bed, shaking his head. "It's a madhouse. My mom was talking in the background while my sister was talking to me. I hope neither one of them loses her sanity by tomorrow." He chuckled.

"Give them a break. It's your sister's day. Like with most brides, I suppose she wants to make sure her day is as perfect as it can be." Turning away from Eric, Sasha bent over and slipped off her heeled knee-high boots. When she stood to take the boots to the closet, she met Eric's mischievous grin.

"Those jeans are something else on you."

"Please," she said, blushing.

"I hope you won't get lonesome while I'm gone."

"I have plenty to keep me occupied. The first thing I'm going to do when you leave is take a long, leisurely bubble bath with a new scent I bought for this trip."

"Oh my goodness. I don't want to leave now. How about I stay and take that tub with you?" He studied her lustfully.

"Nope. Your family needs you, and you have errands to run. I won't be responsible for making them angry. If I were you, I would fear for my life between this evening and the wedding tomorrow. You have promises you've got to fulfill."

Smiling at her, he hooked his arm around her waist and pulled her to him. He kissed her long and hard. "I did tell you how glad I am you came with me, right?"

Held close against him, Sasha could feel his sexual arousal. She reached in to get another taste of his lips. Making the trip with him had made her feel free and wanton. She held him in a tight embrace, relishing the feel of his strong body and wishing they had time for more than tantalizing kisses.

Eric's cell rang again. He swore, seeing it was the neurotic bride. "Yes, Ashley," he answered impatiently without releasing Sasha.

"Yes, I will stop and take care of that too for you on my way to the house. I'm on my way now," he said in a clipped tone, then hung up.

Holding Sasha and gazing with yearning in his eyes, he said, "I hate to leave, babe, but I'd better, before I won't be able to and then I'm going to really have issues."

Sasha giggled and dragged him to the door. "We'll have time to be together tonight. Go on."

He stole one final kiss. "Call me if you need anything."

"Go on. I'm okay. I've been looking after myself for a while, sir. After my bath, I'm going to order some room service and read." She opened the door and playfully pushed him out.

"Whenever I get the chance, I'll call you from the bridal hell zone." He winked and was gone.

In his absence, Sasha did indeed luxuriate in a steamy bubble bath. She lay there thinking over her day and how stressful it had gotten with Trey. She wasn't worried about Craig. She knew that though Trey may have been insensitive by not keeping in touch, she could see that he was definitely glad to be reunited with his son.

Then her mind fell on Eric Prince and how sexy and sweet he had been to her. She respected him for having been so patient with her and allowing her to build trust in him. Soaking her body in the lavender-scented bubbles, she thought of how much she looked forward to his return later.

She couldn't remember the last time she had had decent sex. She'd had a couple of bad dates set up by well-meaning friends and coworkers. Bursting with sexual tension, she had given herself to one guy during a one-night stand that she had later come to regret. She knew she wasn't the kind of woman who could indulge in casual sex without any romance or love attached.

* * *

It was 1:30 a.m. when Sasha got a call from Eric. She had fallen asleep on top of the covers of her bed.

"Say it's not too late for me to come to your room. I'm worn out from being bossed around and socializing with relatives. I was even at the bachelor party, but I got bored. I kept thinking of you alone in that cozy room."

"Hmm. That's impressive," she said in a sexy, drowsy tone. "It's not too late. I can't wait to see you."

"I am the luckiest guy in the world. I'm on my way."

Bounding off the bed, Sasha rushed to the mirror in her room and gently ran a brush through her hair. Then she hurried to the bathroom and rinsed her mouth with mouthwash.

Sasha had no sheer, sexy nightwear. She had considered buying a few pieces for the trip, but she didn't want Eric to think she'd been planning a seduction. Yet the new sleeping attire she wore clung to her figure in all the right places, and she knew Eric would be turned on when he discovered she wasn't wearing any underwear.

When she heard a light rap at the door, she grabbed her terry cloth robe and slipped it on and opened the door.

Seeing Eric filling the doorway, wearing an infectious grin and a smoldering look in his heavenly eyes, she gasped as though she were seeing him for the first time. Just staring at him and how sexy he was dressed in khaki slacks and a designer blue-and-white striped shirt covered by his short leather jacket took her body temperature up a couple of notches.

His eyes gleamed, studying her. Without saying a word, he strolled into the room and enfolded her in his arms and kicked the door shut with one foot. Then he reached behind him and locked it.

While Eric's eager mouth possessed her lips, her body tingled from the warmth and strength of his embrace. Breaking the kiss, she gazed up at him and grinned. "What a greeting," she said, sighing and holding his waist.

Eric placed his finger under her chin. "I don't think we should play games. We each know what the other really wants."

In the next minute she felt his hands beneath her robe, cupping her bottom and pulling her against his erection. The bulge caused her to grow hot and moist where their bodies were pressed together.

Suddenly, she was lifted off her feet and into Eric's arms while he managed to maintain a teasing kiss. Meeting the smoldering look in his eyes, she wrapped her legs around his hips and looped her arms around his neck as he carried her to the bed and laid her down.

Eyeing her with a lustful glow, he began to remove his clothes as hurriedly as he could.

Without any qualms, she too came out of her loungewear. Once Sasha saw him completely disrobed, she leered at his splendid form and thought it was going to fit with hers perfectly.

Eric left several condoms on the nightstand and climbed onto the bed with her. He moved above her and proceeded to taste her lips in a slow and languid manner, caressing her flesh.

All the while the blood in Sasha's veins sizzled throughout her body. She moaned lowly and sweetly as his lips and tongue took hold of first one nipple and then the other. Shivering with delight from his thrills, she ran her hand over the waves of his hair and whispered his name. Feeling his pulsating member pressing near her dewy feminine essence, she parted her thighs as he decorated her neck and shoulders with feathery kisses.

Rolling from one side of the bed to the other, they kissed, caressed, and touched each other with steamy breathing and probing tongues.

Slowly, Eric dragged two fingers back and forth over her glistening wetness, and a trembling Sasha sighed loudly.

After Eric had covered himself with a condom, he grabbed and lifted her bottom and impaled her with a luscious plunge.

Feeling him deep inside her, Sasha gripped herself tightly around his rod. Eric was breathing heavily, groaning and grunting. The sounds of his gratification elevated her even more and mesmerized her with the beautiful, passionate journey they'd embarked upon. Reveling in his steady driving tempo, she matched it. The exquisite motions and harmony of their bodies made her misty-eyed.

Sasha shifted her body forward and pressed her legs against his well-toned hips, her moans now contented whimpers of glee. Her headiness mounted even more as Eric sought her breasts with his hands, and then with his lips and tongue. She thought she would pass out from the joy within her body and soul.

With him stroking her faster and deeper, Sasha's breathing became labored, and she groaned loudly.

Soon they lost all restraint, and their bodies whipped wildly together. Eric let out a curse, then her name, and Sasha returned his call with his name, surrendering her all to him as the two of them drowned in full-bodied ecstatic climaxes.

In the afterglow of their lovemaking, they lay together and laughed softly. They'd found the perfect magic.

Sasha's heart bubbled with happiness as she spooned in bed with Eric, holding his hand and intertwining her fingers with his.

Eric raised himself up on his elbow and gazed at her. He brought their united hands to his lips and kissed the back of her hand.

"This was more than I imagined. It was so wonderful, it scares me. You do realize this changes the dynamics of our relationship. This was more than sex for me; it was a uniting of our hearts and souls."

Sasha responded in a drowsy, sultry tone, "I feel as though I was making love for the first time. Everything felt exciting and new. Until now, I'd been so afraid to let down my guard and really give all to another man. After my marriage failed and then the divorce, I worried I wouldn't be able to please a man and—"

Eric placed his finger over her lips. "Shh. That's the past, and it's done." He smiled. "You're one hell of a woman, Sasha Michaels. You're a loving and sensual woman." He groaned with pleasure. "Oh yes, you are." He hooked the back of her neck and delivered a probing kiss.

At the end of the kiss, he rested his forehead against hers. "Are you ready to move forward in life with me? We can make a new beginning for ourselves. There's only one rule. We must leave all the baggage from our previous relationships and divorces in the past."

She rolled on her back and faced him. "I agree," she said, holding the compelling look in his eyes.

Eric brushed her face with the back of his hand. "What are you thinking about?"

"If you and I are a couple, you're going to have to understand that Craig will be my priority as well. I can't afford for him to think he may be set aside."

"I'm going to have to compete with a fourteen-year-old, huh?"

"This doesn't have to be a competition."

"Easy, Sasha. I was only messing with you. I have no issues with that. In fact, I'd like to bond with him . . . be his friend. The last thing on my mind is disrupting what you have with Craig."

"I'm relieved you feel that way. It'll make being with you that much more meaningful." Stretching as though she were a sensual cat, Sasha locked eyes with Eric, who was watching every curve, every wiggle of her sweet body.

"We've done enough talking." Eric pulled her closer to him and kissed her on the side of her neck. "Let's cuddle and play some more before we sleep."

The tickly feeling of his tongue and mouth on her neck made her giggle. She halted him for a moment and looked at him. "I'm beginning to feel nervous about meeting your family. What if they don't like me?"

"They will like you, Sasha. How can they not like a beautiful, bright woman with such a magnetic personality like yours?" He chortled.

Sasha's face glowed with amusement. "Are you patronizing me, Eric Prince?"

"No. Never. Seriously, baby, you'll be fine. I'm sure they're going to like you. And I want you to know that even if they don't, which I doubt, I do. I make my own decisions concerning my life." Eric embraced her and kissed her tenderly and sweetly.

Sasha clung to his broad shoulders and indulged herself in the raw, sweet passion of the moment.

Ending the kisses to taste the tips of her breasts with flicks of his tongue, Eric felt Sasha's skin turn hot. He ran his hand from the curve of her waist to her hips, to the curve of her luscious thighs. The moment he touched her moist female essence, she let out a blissful moan and went limp as his long, strong fingers worked magic within her.

Soon Eric was above her and inside her, thrilling her with his steellike hardness, and immediately they fell into a hypnotic tempo.

Feeling as though her center would burst from the sensation of Eric's wondrous motions, her heart galloping in her chest, Sasha let out a shout of gratification. She hugged his waist and ordered him to move faster. He caught up to her, and then they both sang in a key of lustful harmony.

The intimate moment had been so intense, it drained them physically. They fell apart and upon their backs, drenched in perspiration, exhaling and inhaling as though they'd been running for their lives.

Sasha turned on her side and reached for Eric's face. She gave him a drowsy look. "You're going to have me addicted to you." She grinned.

"And you're most definitely my drug of choice," he said, fondling her round, shapely bottom.

As their bodies cooled to the temperature of the room, the two of them settled beneath the covers, and Sasha closed her eyes, relishing their newfound closeness. Quickly they fell asleep in each other's arms in the cozy nest of the bed.

Chapter 11

Sasha Michaels had attended many weddings, but she hadn't ever seen one as spectacular as Ashley Prince's. The one o'clock event took place in a huge cathedral that had been decorated in the most breathtaking manner, with all kinds of beautiful flowers and candles. There were at least three hundred guests, many of them dignitaries from the political scene in Washington, D.C., and the black upper crust of northern Virginia.

Sitting on the side of the church with the bride's family, Sasha could feel herself becoming nervous among Eric's impressive-looking family members and friends. *How could a woman like me, who grew up in a blue-collar neighborhood, fit into this world of privilege?*

After the wedding, she was glad to meet up with Miles. He'd caught her off guard, taking her by the arm.

"Eric told me to look out for you. He asked me to take you to the wedding reception. He has to stay here for a while. They have pictures they want to get of the wedding party."

"Fine by me. I'm so glad to see a familiar face," Sasha said, relieved she didn't have to stand around alone and feel out of her element.

Holding on to her arm and escorting her to the parking lot where his car was, Miles greeted several people.

"I can't get over that wedding. It's something I thought I'd only see in a movie. I had no idea Eric and his family had it like that," Sasha said once Miles settled in behind the wheel of his car.

"You wouldn't believe it from how down-to-earth Eric is, would you? I remember getting my first time of the high life Eric lived. When we became friends in college, he invited me home with him for a weekend. I couldn't get over the fabulous mansion he brought me to. All the while he and I were hanging out on campus, I thought he was just another around-the-way dude. Come to find out, the kid attended private schools, golfed, and had traveled the world a couple of times with his family. The weekend I visited with the Princes, I heard them have conversations about well-known people they were cool with. I mean, the people they spoke of are the kind you read about in magazines and see on television, and they were friendly with them."

"I'm nervous about meeting his family. Suppose

they don't like me? I certainly don't want to cause any friction in his family."

"You won't have anything to worry about, Sasha. They're going to like you as much as Eric does." Miles grinned.

"How much has Eric told you about us?"

"He's told me enough to let me know that he's crazy about you. And you've changed the man in the couple months you two have been seeing each other. You've particularly ruined the bond of friendship he and I had. I mean, we used to hang out at the clubs and run game on women." Miles dabbed his eyes with his handkerchief, feigning tears. "I'm alone now. I have no one to play with."

"Quit it, Miles. You are too much." Sasha laughed at his antics.

Miles informed her the reception would take place in one of the large ballrooms at the Marriott.

"I'm going to fix my face," she informed Miles when they reached the hotel. "Don't get too far away. You're the only person I know. I need you today." She grinned at him. "I thought I'd never hear myself telling you that." She removed her coat and handed it to Miles to check along with his.

"Go do what you got to. I'll be here in the lobby, seeing which of these lovely ladies I can get close to." He walked off behind a tall, statuesque young woman, who looked like a model or an actress.

Sasha knew she was going to have to get a glass

of wine once they hit the reception. Her nerves needed to be smoothed out. Hustling into the bathroom, she went to one of the stalls to handle the water she'd been holding for what seemed like forever, and heard several other women filling up the lounge area of the restroom.

Sasha found space at one of the many mirrors in the lounge area to touch up her hair and face. She wasn't pleased that the blustery wind had mussed her hair. She pulled out her comb to set it back in order. Next she pulled out her MAC cosmetics and tried to touch up her face the way the artist at the Nordstrom counter had instructed.

Two women close to her age entered the area and went to the mirror on the other side of the room. They could have been some of Ashley's friends or the daughters of some of the highbrow acquaintances of Mr. and Mrs. Prince. While Sasha retouched her makeup, she picked up on the conversation the women were having.

"I can't believe how fine Eric Prince looks now," the one with the bob hairstyle said.

"It a shame how he has gotten dreamier than ever. Just think, he was my first love," the tall, pretty one said.

"That was one hot high school romance. You two held on to each other for two years."

"We sure did. I had my first of everything with him. He and I certainly have some good memories."

"It's a shame that you two went off to separate

colleges. Who knows what fate would have had in store for you? Just think, you and he could have been one of those power couples—two medical doctors. You could have been Dr. Gabrielle Ryan-Prince." The woman laughed.

Gabrielle sighed. "That's true, Jillian. I'd been primed to be a physician from the time I was in middle school. I wanted to make my father proud by following in his footsteps, so I chose internal medicine, like him. Now I'm sharing his practice with him, and the two of us love working together."

"And, remember, when Eric went off to college, that spoiled brat, Lorene, got a hold of him and convinced him he loved her enough to marry her."

"Circumstances and distance were the reasons Eric and I drifted apart. I was excited about attending Howard University. Between maintaining my grades and dating when I could, I had my hands full. Remember, I even began dating that theater major from the Caribbean."

"That accent of his won you completely over. You two were a couple for a while too."

"We were serious. I dumped Eric for that brother. At the time, he seemed to be more sophisticated and mature than Eric. He graduated and went to Europe to study further, and that was that for us. I threw myself into my studies and dated when I had the time. I had another serious boyfriend for a short while, but I had to get him out of my life. He was entirely too tiresome for me." Gabrielle leaned in close to the mirror to apply lipstick. "Seeing Eric in the wedding as an usher, looking elegant as an actor who walks the red carpet, I felt those sweet, old feelings I had for him when I was a teen. I suppose it's like that old saying, you never forget your first love." She sighed and placed her hand over her heart. "I remember the summer nights of making out, walking on the beach, or simply hanging out in the mall and holding hands and just being loved by him. I wish I could turn back the hands of time and be that girl—his girl again."

"If I didn't know better, I would think you're interested in picking up where you left off. You could have another chance. After all, he is divorced and available from the latest I've heard from people who know him. I understand that when his marriage ended, he kind of turned into a player. If I had been married to that selfish Lorene, I would probably come out of my bag and have some fun. He probably caught hell trying to please her. You know, her parents always made sure she had the best of everything. I can't imagine her being married and having to compromise her wants and needs to a man who tried to be her husband."

"Tell me about her. I don't know what Eric could have been thinking. She must have put on some kind of act to rein him in the way she did."

"It's over now. Since he's out of that toxic

relationship, he looks better. He still has that disarming smile that used to make all the women weak. I see that sparkle in your eyes. I have a feeling you're going to try to make a connection with him."

"I wish. It certainly would be the right time for me. I'm available. But he might have someone he's seeing, so I shouldn't dare to get my hopes up."

"Hold up. The Gabrielle I know would welcome the challenge of working her way back into his life. I was sitting close enough to see the front of the church during the ceremony. I didn't see a wedding band on his finger. You know what they say, all is fair in love and war."

"Jillian, you are too much." Gabrielle laughed. Then she stood back from the mirror to check out the simple black dress that looked perfect on her shapely body. "Let's go. You know I'm going out of my way to say hello to him and see what he has going on in his life."

"You must. You can't let this opportunity pass you by."

The two women sashayed out of the ladies' room with an air of confidence that made them even more striking in appearance.

After the women left, Sasha took a seat in a chair, ill at ease from what she'd heard and seen. She popped a piece of peppermint in her mouth. Doubts filled her mind. What if seeing Gabrielle again today awakened the emotions he had shared with her as his first love? Sasha couldn't deny that Dr. Gabrielle Ryan was a stunning woman. Plus, she was a physician. Also, she had come from his background, had never been married, and had no children, from what Sasha heard. In Sasha's mind, Gabrielle could prove to be competition for her, particularly in this setting among Eric's family and friends.

Whenever she was with Eric, she was the one who always brought up the differences in their background. Eric had told her he didn't care about where she'd lived or her mother's misfortune. His interest was in the woman Sasha had become in spite of that and her failed marriage.

Sasha told herself she was being ridiculous. She took a deep breath. Didn't Eric tell her he cared for her? Something he emphasized even more in the sweet and passionate way they'd made love the night before. With these thoughts in mind, she straightened her outfit and went out to find Miles and to join the other guests until Eric could be by her side.

Chapter 12

Eric hadn't been able to get with Sasha until halfway through the wedding reception. That was after all the pictures had been taken, the video had been made, and the bride and groom had been toasted. Then there were the required dances of the bridal party and the parents of the bride and groom. The program part of the reception was touching and full of beautiful sentiment.

Sasha watched Eric as he danced with the petite bridesmaid. Miles had informed Sasha that the bridesmaid was married and in the early stages of pregnancy. Everyone thought Eric and the young woman made a humorous couple, with him being an obstetrician.

Eric made his way across the room with a flute of champagne. He took a seat at the table with Miles and Sasha and sat beside Sasha. He kissed her on the lips and smiled.

"I've tried not to complain or whine about anything I've been asked to do," Eric said. "But I'm done. I'm glad her day is just about up. I can't take any more from Ashley or my mom." He took a big gulp of his champagne. "I'm so glad to have you guys here. I can relax and be down. I've smiled and talked so much with family and friends of the family, my face aches." He chortled.

Sasha touched his face. "Poor baby."

He grinned at Sasha. "Now it's your turn. I want you to meet my parents. I've mentioned you to them, and they're looking forward to seeing you."

Sasha's stomach twisted in knots. She'd seen the regal couple, Meredith and Webster Prince, and dreaded being introduced. She feared making a bad impression. She'd imagined herself stumbling over her words or not being able to have a decent conversation with them. She was intimidated by the fact that his parents were considered the cream of the black community in the area and also well respected in most of northern Virginia and the D.C. area.

When a waiter approached the table with champagne, Sasha reached for a serving and drank almost half of it for the courage she was looking for.

His arm around Sasha's chair, Eric said to Miles, "I can imagine you've been having fun checking out all the women here. There are quite a few available professional women here for you to choose from."

"I've been checking them out. A few are interesting, but some are on the chilly side. My game doesn't work on them like it does on the women in Huntersville. They aren't as eager to get with a brother like me. Can you believe how these sisters have damaged my ego?" He feigned hurt.

Sasha laughed. "Some of these women are a bit too classy for me and you."

"Hold up. Why are you guys picking on my crowd? They're okay. Once you get to know them, they're all good."

"My man, I don't have time to chip away at the ice walls these women have built around them. It's not that serious. I only came because I promised you I would. And I like your sister. She knows she should have been marrying me today." Miles pressed his tie with his hand and brushed the shoulders of his suit. "I think I'm finer than that dude she married."

Eric laughed. "You had a crush on her, but I dared you to say anything out of the way to her. I knew what a dawg you were. I wasn't having you messing over my sister."

"I respected you too. That was a tragic situation. She wanted me, but you kept us from hooking up."

"Man, you're crazy. My sister was dating some football quarterback in those days. She couldn't see or hear anyone but him back then."

"She certainly looks happy with her new husband," Sasha said, admiring the newlywed couple as they mingled with the guests. "She's a gorgeous bride. That dress she has on is elegant and stunning on her."

"You didn't mention how I look. My feelings are hurt." He took Sasha's hand.

"You are the best-looking man in the wedding party," Sasha gushed. "Not only did I notice that, but I could see several other sisters eyeing you as well."

"Enough of this flattery. I'm going to the bar to see if I can find some hard liquor instead of this bubbly champagne." Miles got up and left Eric and Sasha alone.

"You look marvelous, baby," Eric said, sizing her up in her outfit. "I still can't get the beauty of your body without clothes out of my mind."

"Eric! Not here. Where are your manners?" Sasha could feel the back of her neck growing warm. Briefly, her thoughts went to Eric's strong nude body erotically massaging hers.

"Aw, look at your face . . . turning rosy." Eric squeezed her shoulder. He gazed across the room where his parents sat, talking to a few guests. "Come on, this is a good time for us to join my folks, so I can introduce you to them." He rose to his full six-foot height and stood behind her.

Sasha leaned her head back and gazed up at him. "I'm nervous."

"Don't. It's going to be okay. I'm going to be right by your side."

Sasha stood and tugged at her outfit. "Maybe I should touch up my makeup, comb my hair."

"You look perfect, Sasha. Let's do this." Eric took her hand and walked with her across the room.

By the time they'd gotten to the elder Princes' table, the other guests had left. The couple smiled at their son and his date as they approached.

"It's just about over, Mom and Dad." Eric touched his mother on the shoulder. "Everything went the way you wanted it to."

"I'm thankful for that," Mrs. Prince said, eyeing Sasha with a pleasant look. "Well, Eric, who is this lovely young woman?"

"Mom, Dad, this is Sasha Michaels. She is one of the nurse supervisors at the hospital where I work. The two of us have begun to date recently. Sasha, my parents, Meredith and Webster Prince."

Mr. Prince rose from his chair and extended his hand to her. "Pleased to meet you. Very pleased." He gave her a warm smile.

Mrs. Prince took her hand as well. "Nice to meet you. Have a seat, dear."

"The same here. Thank you," Sasha said, taking the chair near his mother that Eric pulled out for her.

"Eric, will you signal that waiter?" Mr. Prince said. "I want another pitcher of cold water for our table."

Eric did as he was told.

"My goodness, Webster, what is it with you and all this water? You've gone through two pitchers alone already. You act as though it's a hundred degrees in here." Mrs. Prince laughed softly.

Mr. Prince placed an arm around his wife's shoulder and smiled at her affectionately. "I love you too. She watches my every move. She shows how much she worships me by picking on me."

"Webster," she said softly, "Eric brought this young lady here for us to chat with, not to listen to us old folks carry on."

Sasha glanced at Eric and smiled. She thought it was adorable the way his parents carried on, making her feel more relaxed in their presence.

In the short time she had been at the table, she could see the resemblance between the two, and that Eric had some of the same mannerisms as his father. Sasha could also see that Eric got his keen handsome features from his mother.

The waiter returned to the table quickly and placed the chilled pitcher in the center of the table. Mr. Webster poured a glassful of water and savored the coolness of his drink as though he was parched dry.

"So, Sasha dear, you work at Hope Hospital? That is wonderful. Did you move there recently to work?" Mrs. Prince asked.

"I grew up in Huntersville. I moved away for a while and moved back after my divorce."

A flash of curiosity flashed in Mrs. Prince's light brown eyes. "You're divorced too." She smiled politely. "You have any children?"

"Yes, I have a son."

"I see," Mrs. Prince said. "You're a single working mom, huh? I can imagine it hasn't been easy with a young son."

"Well, it used to be rather difficult, but my son is fourteen and quite independent, thankfully."

Mrs. Prince's eyes widened at the mention of a teen son.

Pouring himself another glass of water, Mr. Prince said, "My goodness, you certainly don't look old enough to have a teenage son."

Suddenly, Sasha felt awkward for having to explain her situation, but she certainly had nothing to be ashamed of. Her life was what it was.

"I married young. I was barely out of high school when I had my son and got married." Sasha, her hands resting in her lap, glanced at Eric as he slipped his hand in hers and held it tightly.

Just then, Ashley and her husband, Brandon, arrived at their table. Ashley required assistance from her groom and Eric to settle her confection of a gown into a chair.

"Mom, I'm tired," Ashley said. "These shoes are fabulous, but my feet are aching."

Mrs. Prince beamed at her daughter. "Well, you look like an angel, sweetheart. And I'm certain your husband will be more than happy to give you a foot massage later."

Everyone laughed.

"Sis, Brandon—or should I say Mr. and Mrs. McCullough now? Anyway, I'd like for you to meet my date, Sasha Michaels."

Ashley met Sasha's gaze. "Hello. I'm glad you could come today."

"Nice to meet one of Eric's dates." Brandon grinned at Eric.

"One? Man, you're trying to start something, and you haven't been in the family but a few hours," Eric said humorously.

"I meant no harm, but you know I really know you, man."

"No, you don't. I've changed. And this lady is responsible." Eric smiled warmly at Sasha.

"It's about time for you to make a change," Ashley said. "I didn't like the things I was hearing about you and your social life."

Eric opened his mouth to defend himself, but his mother cut him off.

"Okay, let's not do this today. We're supposed to be a big happy family today."

The next thing Sasha knew, Gabrielle Ryan appeared at their table. "Hello, family," she said cheerily. "I had to come over to let you know how great everything has been. And I wanted to say hello to this one." She eyed Eric. "You've been avoiding me, haven't you?"

Eric jumped to his feet and went to embrace her. Sasha watched the way he held his first love, closing his eyes as he took her in his arms. She wondered if he was reliving the memories of their romance. She pushed the jealous thoughts out of her mind, deciding she had nothing to do with the history the two of them shared.

"It's good to see you, Gabrielle. I've been meaning to catch up to you, but these ladies have all kept me busy with one thing or another."

"Gabrielle, how are your mother and father? I'm sorry they couldn't join us today. Give them my regards and tell them Webster and I will be in New York soon. We can't wait to see that new condo they've moved into."

"I sure will, Mrs. Prince," Gabrielle said, clinging to Eric's arm as though he were her man. "Remember when Eric and I were the hot teen couple? Back then, I used to dream of being his bride."

"How can I forget? Your mother and I had crossed our fingers on that idea. It was nice knowing the family and the background and not having to worry over either of you being with the wrong person," Mrs. Prince said. "But you kids had your own goals and ambitions that drove you apart. I'm extremely proud of you, Gabrielle. You've become a role model for young women of color, being an internist and a surgeon, not to mention the motivational speaking you do when you can, and your mentoring program for young girls interested in becoming physicians."

Sasha took offense. Did Mrs. Prince resent the idea of her son dating a woman who was only a nurse? She also wondered if Mrs. Prince felt she wasn't the proper woman for her son after learning of Sasha's marriage as a teen.

"Eric, go get that photographer," Mrs. Prince

said. "We must all take a picture together with Gabrielle. She's so much like family to us."

While Eric was away, Gabrielle took his seat and smiled politely at Sasha. "Hi, I'm Gabrielle Ryan."

"I'm Sasha Michaels."

"Are you a relative? I thought I'd met most of the people in the Prince family at one time or another."

"Sasha is Eric's date." Mr. Prince took a gulp of his ice water. "She works as a nurse at Hope Hospital in Huntersville with Eric."

The warmth in Gabrielle's face faded a bit. "How interesting." She turned her attention to Ashley and her groom and began discussing the plans the two had for their honeymoon in Saint-Tropez.

Eric returned to the table, the eager photographer in tow. "Here he is, everybody. Come on and let's stand to make a nice group shot."

Sasha didn't move. She knew she wasn't family and didn't want to intrude. *If they want me in the picture, they'll say so.*

Sasha was envious and a bit hurt as she watched Eric and his family pose. Not only did Eric not ask her to join them, but he insisted that Gabrielle stand beside him. And Gabrielle placed an arm around his waist, and he matched her action. Sasha couldn't deny that Eric and Gabrielle looked quite excited to be together again.

After several shots were taken, they all stood together, chatting and laughing. Sasha felt like an outsider and began to doubt if Eric was really serious about her. After seeing his old girlfriend, he might want to reestablish what they had started in their youth.

Sasha sat, sipping champagne and eating a piece of wedding cake, feeling more envious the longer Eric spoke and laughed with Gabrielle. She watched Dr. Ryan toss her long caramel-blond hair flirtatiously and grin at him until her light complexion glowed. The woman was acting as though she longed to spend more time with him alone.

Sasha's attention was diverted from Eric when she noticed Mr. Prince stagger away from the group. His color wasn't good at all, and he clutched his chest in a grimace, then collapsed unconscious on the floor.

Sasha bolted from her seat and rushed over to Mr. Prince, dropping to her knees to feel his pulse at his neck and wrist. She rolled him on his back to free him of his tie and ripped open his shirt to begin the process of resuscitation.

In the midst of her actions, Eric and Gabrielle rushed over. "Call EMS," Gabrielle ordered Sasha.

Despite his distraught look, Eric took over from Sasha. Gasping with fear, Mrs. Prince hovered near her husband, and the whole room of guests gathered around with curious and concerned expressions.

"Daddy! Oh, Daddy!" Ashley wept and clung to Brandon.

After calling for assistance, Sasha went to Mrs.

Prince and placed a soothing arm around her and helped her to a chair.

All the while, Eric, his face drenched with perspiration, and fear in his eyes, hovered above his father and worked on him to get his heart beating. Then a glimmer of joy flashed in his eyes. "I got a heartbeat!"

Gabrielle joined Eric, and they discussed the situation among themselves.

Easing up beside Eric, who looked dazed, Sasha attempted to take his hand, but he didn't accept it. He turned away from her and went to his mother, who sat sobbing, and whispered into her ear while he held her.

While Sasha stood outside the family circle and watched, the paramedics came bursting into the room with a gurney. They were met by the take-charge Dr. Ryan, who shot off Webster Prince's vitals.

After the paramedics lifted Mr. Prince onto the gurney to transport him to the hospital, Dr. Ryan called out to Eric.

Miles eased up behind Sasha and placed a caring hand on her shoulder. "What's the matter with Mr. Prince?" he asked her quietly.

"Cardiac arrest. I noticed he couldn't seem to get enough cold water while I was at their table. Usually, that's a sign when people have serious heart issues. I suppose all the stress and hustle to pull off his daughter's wedding must have taken him down. He probably had been having signs, but was ignoring them, I bet," she said, watching Eric and Gabrielle rushing behind the gurney.

Eric turned toward Sasha as though he had just remembered her. "I'll call you later."

"I've got her, man," Miles told him.

Eric forced an appreciative smile and made his way out of the room. And Sasha and Miles followed them out to the emergency vehicle, where other guests had gathered as well.

Eric and Gabrielle vanished inside the vehicle.

Soon Ashley, her veil removed and in hand, and Brandon followed, holding Mrs. Prince's hands. Then the emergency vehicle, its red and blue lights flashing, pulled off and rushed into the traffic.

Sasha wondered if she should get Miles to take her to the hospital. But then she decided she would only be in the way. And Eric had told her he would call. She decided to ask Miles to take her back to her hotel room, where she would wait for Eric to call her to let her know what she could do for him and his family at this awful time.

Sasha longed to be with Eric, but she didn't want to come off as a nuisance. Seeing the distraught look on his face, she wanted to hold him, to ease his fears, but Eric's family needed him. She thought the best thing for her to do was to stay out of the way until the situation improved.

Chapter 13

After all the excitement had cleared, Miles took Sasha to her hotel room. He had decided to go to the hospital to see how things were going and had offered to take her as they left the reception, but she decided against it.

Once she was inside her room, Sasha realized how emotionally drained she was by all that had occurred. She changed into her loungewear and lay across her bed with the television on for company. Soon, she drifted off into a deep sleep.

Awakened by the ringing cell phone she had clutched in her hand, she sat up and flipped the phone on.

She was relieved to hear Eric's voice. "Eric, I'm so glad you've finally called. I've been so concerned. How is your father?"

"Thanks, babe," he said in a weary tone. "My dad is in surgery. He's having a triple bypass. Can you believe that? He hasn't been complaining or anything. He exercises nearly every day at his gym, and he's been watching his diet lately."

"I'm sure he's going to be fine. How's the family?"

"Everyone is a wreck. My sister only took off her wedding gown a couple of hours ago. Everyone is staked out in the waiting room until the surgery is over."

"Is there anything I can do?"

"We're good for now. I saw you rushing to help him. We're grateful."

"I didn't do anything I wasn't trained to do."

"Hey, I'm not going to be able to drive back tomorrow. I'm going to hang out with my family for the remainder of the week, help monitor my dad's condition. Gabrielle will be here as well. She's taken a couple of weeks off. She was planning a vacation but decided to change her reservations until next week."

"Oh . . . okay," Sasha responded slowly. She figured Gabrielle was using the opportunity to get closer with Eric again. She hated herself for thinking that way, but she knew how women were. Gabrielle impressed her as the kind of woman who, when she saw something she wanted, went after it until it was hers.

"Miles will be leaving tomorrow too. He said you're more than welcome to ride back to Huntersville with him."

"I'm going to have to take him up on that. I

have to get home to meet Craig and his father. Will I have a chance to say good-bye to you before I leave?"

"Sure. If everything turns out good here, I'll be coming by the hotel in the morning to see you off."

"I'm glad to hear that. Since we're going to be apart for a while, I would love to hold you and kiss you until we can be together again."

Eric laughed softly. "I could use some of your lovin' about now. I'm going to tell Miles you want that ride. He'll probably call you later, so you two can decide when to leave. Don't worry about your bill. I've already taken care of that."

"Thanks. The wedding was lovely. It was a pleasure to meet your family. There are still plenty of good memories to treasure from this."

"I suppose. It was a great day until . . . well, you know . . ."

"Yeah, I do. This is life. It has its tests."

"You're right about that. Well, I'm going to say good night. I'll be by in the morning."

"Call me, if you need me."

"Thanks."

"Eric, I love you."

For a moment, he was quiet. "I needed to hear that."

There was a hesitation. Then Sasha recognized Gabrielle's voice in the background, telling Eric that the doctor would be down soon.

"I have to go," he said hurriedly. "I'll see you tomorrow."

Sasha flipped off her phone and sat on the side of the bed, wishing she had been there with him. She didn't like the idea of Gabrielle hanging around as though she were a member of the family. Yet there was nothing she could do about that. She turned off the light and climbed into bed, praying for the Prince family, and for Eric and their new relationship.

On the drive from Eric's hometown with Miles, Sasha was miffed. Although Miles tried to keep her attention with conversation, she wasn't in the mood to hear what he had to say.

That morning she was looking forward to having a few moments alone with Eric before she hit the road, but he came to the hotel with Gabrielle, who had come to her room, but then waited downstairs in the hotel lobby, drinking coffee and reading the morning paper. Gabrielle had spent the night at the Princes' home, and Eric was giving her a ride to the hotel she'd been booked in.

Sasha was glad to learn that Eric's father had made it through the surgery and that he had a good prognosis. She and Eric shared kisses and embraces.

The stress of his father's illness could be seen in Eric's demeanor. He was quiet with Sasha, who tried to remind herself he was this way because he was going through a serious situation. She would have dealt with Eric's tepid behavior better if Gabrielle wasn't in tow and she hadn't learned that his mother had invited Gabrielle to stay at their home with them while her husband recuperated in the hospital.

Eric told her that after his father's surgery was complete and the doctor had assured them he would be fine, everyone encouraged Ashley and Brandon to go on their honeymoon. And Webster had assured Ashley that he would be back on his feet by the time they returned.

Knowing that Gabrielle was in the lobby, Sasha and Eric shared their good-bye kisses and hugs. He'd vowed to call her and to keep in touch until he could return to Huntersville.

"Sasha, you're not listening to a word I'm saying," Miles said, breaking her reverie.

"I am listening to you." She feigned a grin.

"No, you aren't. I've been testing you. I made up a story about how I had made out with two bridesmaids at the same time in my room. All you said was, 'That's interesting, Miles.' I didn't know you had a little freak in you." He laughed.

Sasha blushed. "Okay, you got me. That wasn't a true story, was it?"

"C'mon, you know me."

"Yeah, I do know you. Ever since your breakup with your lady, I don't know what to expect. And you certainly made a lot of connections with the females at the wedding."

"I had no threesome. That's just one of my fantasies." He chuckled. "Gabrielle Ryan got on your nerves tagging along with Eric, didn't she?"

"To be honest, she did. Did he tell you she would be a guest in his family home while he's there too?"

"Yep. I know." Miles eyed her.

"That bothers me. The two of them had a relationship, you know."

"Yes, I know that too. They were kids. That was years ago, Sasha. I don't think you have anything to worry over."

"Tell me what you know about Gabrielle. I'm pretty sure Eric shared that part of his life with you."

Miles smiled. "You're really serious about my man. He's got you all jealous . . . vulnerable and stuff."

"Why do I have to be that? I merely was interested in their relationship." Sasha folded her arms and looked out the window, away from him.

"All I know is that they were as serious as any teenagers could be. You know how it is when you share all those firsts with someone. Those first kisses that make you feel like a man, or a woman in your case, the feeling of belonging to someone, the struggle of fighting with your hormones not to take it to that ultimate level and—"

"I get it, Miles. I've known people who have found their first love and rekindled that passion."

"I don't think you have that to worry about. Gabrielle is no longer that cute little cheerleader Eric shared puppy love with. You met her. Honestly, her personality has changed and not for the better. She is arrogant and has lost that softness Eric likes in his women."

Hearing that didn't make Sasha feel any better. She remembered how happy Eric appeared to be when he saw Gabrielle. Now that they were thrown together by the crisis, the two might be interested in putting the pieces together.

"Sasha, I see the anxiety on your face. Don't worry. Eric's coming back to you."

"I'm all right, Miles. I'm not worried. I was merely trying to make conversation."

"Right," Miles answered, chuckling.

"When it gets right down to it for me, the only male I should concern myself with is the one I'm raising. He's my priority right now."

Miles grinned. "Whatever, Sasha."

"Since you and I can't have a decent discussion, turn the radio up. I'm going to take a nap the rest of the way home." Sasha closed her eyes and threw her head back on the headrest.

Sasha longed to speak with Eric, to hear his soothing voice, but she was determined not to call him and be a nuisance. She could only hope he would call later in the evening and calm some of the doubts that she couldn't lay to rest.

Chapter 14

It was nearly three o'clock in the day when Craig burst through the door, struggling with his bags. Sasha had been home for a couple of hours and had spent her time straightening the house from the mess she and Craig had left before going their separate ways for the weekend.

Staring at her son as he dropped everything near the door, she walked towards him with a smile. "Hey, baby." She went to greet him and to help him move his bags out of the passageway. "Where's my hug?" She opened her arms to him. He filled her arms and hugged tightly. She held him at arm's length. "You and I have been away from each other for a few days, but I swear you look as though you've grown a bit." She pulled him to her again. "I'm glad you're home."

"Mom, what did you bring me from your trip?"

She shook her head. "Is that all you're concerned about? Didn't you miss me a little bit?"

Craig stared at his mother with a grin. "Yeah, I did. But did you buy anything?"

"I didn't get a chance to go out shopping like I planned. I did shop in the hotel tourist store and bought you a hooded shirt with *Virginia is for Lovers* on it."

He gave her a questioning look.

"It's black with a red heart," Sasha said, defending her gift. "I figured you were old enough to consider yourself a lover. How about that?" She laughed.

"Cool. I like that, Mom."

Trey entered the house with a couple of shopping bags. "Sasha, I brought our son back to you all in one piece." He reached for Craig and gripped the back of his neck playfully.

Sasha took Trey's coat and offered him a seat. "Was he a good guest?"

"Karen and I didn't consider him a guest. He's family to us. You should have seen how well he and his twin brothers got along. Karen got a break with him around. She taught him how take care of the kids, and he took right to it."

Craig took a seat on the floor near them and clicked the television on with the remote control.

Sasha stared at him. "You had fun, huh?"

"Mom, you got to see my brothers. I can't wait until they get bigger, so I can teach them stuff.

Dad took pictures of us. He promised to e-mail them to me when he gets a chance."

Hearing her son, Sasha realized she had to get used to the idea of the other part of his family pulling him into their life. Wasn't this what she wanted for Craig? But seeing how well Trey and Craig had gotten along for the first weekend in a long time together, Sasha feared she would be replaced. A growing boy such as Craig needed his father at this time in his life. She knew young men didn't want to grow up being mama's boys.

"Sasha, you look more relaxed since the last time I saw you. Your trip must have been really great."

"I had fun. I went to a wedding with—with a friend. It was lavish yet beautiful. And, of course, it was good to get out of town for a few days."

Craig was watching a football game on television, and he and his father began to cheer and talk about the players.

"Would you guys like something to drink or eat? I have a feeling Craig probably wants something."

"I could use a sandwich, Mom."

"Well, you can fix it for yourself. There's plenty of deli meat in the fridge. Take your father's order too."

Craig looked surprised. "I thought you were serving me."

"No. You keep telling me not to baby you. If I wait on you hand and foot, that would be babying you." Sasha chuckled.

Craig got up from the floor. "Dad, you want a sandwich too?"

"No, son. I'll take a soft drink, though. I'm going to be hitting the road in thirty minutes."

"I got you," Craig said as he swaggered into the kitchen.

Once Craig had left the room, Sasha could feel Trey watching her. Out of the corner of her eye she could tell from the expression on his face that there was something on his mind.

In the next moment, Trey cleared his throat to get her attention and he sat on the edge of the chair. "Sasha, I have something I'd like to discuss with you. I want you to hear me out, before you say a word," he said, his tone somber.

Seeing the serious look, Sasha felt her stomach clenching tight with nervousness. "What's going on, Trey?"

He rubbed his hands together. "I'm going to start by complimenting you on the wonderful job you've done of raising Craig. I'm so proud of the sensitive and caring kid he is. I'm proud to have a son like him."

Sasha didn't respond to his comment. In fact, she wanted to remind him that she had practically raised him on her own since he had little or no time for Craig when he was a little kid. To her, Trey only began to take an interest in Craig in the last couple of years. He waited until the boy was nearly self-sufficient and nearly a man to be an integral part of his life. Though she had forgiven

Trey, she couldn't forget how self-centered he had been when they were together with their young son. Consumed with his career and social climbing, Trey believed that meeting all the right people in his field would be his key to success.

"There's no need for you to look surly." Trey smiled nervously.

"Just say what you have to say, Trey."

Rubbing the side of his face, Trey lowered his eyes. "What would you say to allowing Craig to live with me? I'd like for him to go to a private school in my area. He tells me basketball is the only thing that's made school bearable for him. He claims he's bored and he has told me how crude and rough some of the guys have been to him. In my opinion, he'll fare better in a private school. It's time for him to prepare for getting into a good college, and this private school where most of my colleagues send their kids will definitely do that."

Stunned, Sasha couldn't speak for a minute. She couldn't believe that, after all the time, effort, and struggle, Trey wanted to just snatch her son out of her life.

"You've got to be kidding me." Sasha crossed her arms, refusing to look at Trey.

"I'm serious. It's obvious you've done all you can for him. You called me and told me about his anger and the trouble in school. I've talked to him, and he doesn't seem to have a problem with my suggestion. Didn't you want me to discuss his issues with him?"

"I did, but I didn't expect you to talk him into running away from his problems."

"Come on, Sasha. It's not about teaching him to run away. It's about doing what's best for him. I can afford to send him to private school."

"Big deal, Trey. I don't feel that letting your money raise him is the answer."

Trey frowned. "You're not being fair. It's not about money, and you know it."

Sasha began to pace from one end of the room to the other. Then she came and stood before Trey. Staring at him defiantly, her arms folded at her waist, she said, "If Craig was ill-mannered and obnoxious, would you want him to come live with you then?"

Trey glowered at her. "Why would you ask something like that when I'm trying to have an intelligent conversation about him?"

The thought of handing Craig over to Trey wasn't anything Sasha was ready to deal with. She had been stressed enough over leaving Eric in the clutches of Gabrielle Ryan.

Noticing how Trey's expression had turned to anger, she bit down on her lip. Fuming, she was reminded of their troubled marriage, with all the heartache, disappointment, loneliness, and feelings of inadequacy she had experienced from that same dissatisfied expression he displayed. When she tried to be the woman he wanted, there wasn't anything she could say or do to please him. It was either his way or no way at all. She was always the one left in tears, left to stress, and feeling as though she was inferior to him.

"Since you're interested in sending him to a private school, he can attend one here in Huntersville. There are plenty of schools you and I can check out together."

"You're missing the point, Sasha. To be honest with you, I want him to live with me. That way I can be a real father to him now. You always hinted he needed me more. I agree with you. This weekend opened my eyes. He's growing up fast, and I'd like for him to be able to say I was in his life. Everyone is always preaching about how black men aren't around for their kids. Here I am, trying to do the right thing by forging a bond with him, and you're trying to deny me that."

She laughed at him. "What you're offering isn't fair to me. I want to continue to be in his life. I loved him before you ever began to take an interest in him."

Trey clenched his mouth tighter. Then he spoke in a controlled tone. "Let's be reasonable. I'm not trying to take your baby from you. We'll just switch the visitation around. You'll get to have Craig on certain holidays, and he can come to you on some weekends when it doesn't interfere with his school assignments or other activities."

Sasha took a seat and tried to calm her nerves. She considered his words, but she wasn't ready to make a commitment. She just couldn't, not at this time. After all, she was dealing with her heart and her blood. Craig had been her priority and responsibility for far too long for her to just hand him over to Trey simply because he decided he was ready to be a real father.

"Look at it this way, Sasha, with Craig out of the house, you'll have a chance to do some of the things that you've denied yourself. My boy told me you have a man you're seeing on a regular basis. Dr. Eric Prince. I've met him a couple times. I have to admit, I'm impressed with your selection. His family is one of the most prestigious, black or white, in northern Virginia."

Sasha swore silently. Craig had told his father way more than she wanted him to.

"I don't care how impressed you are. And don't tell me what I should be doing with my life, so you can take my child away from me." She had to catch her breath, because she was talking faster than usual. "I don't believe you're going to be that much different with Craig, should he live with you. I bet you probably figured if he went to school with your highbrow associates, you and your wife have even more reason to be closer with them. I bet you and she are already making plans for Craig to get in with all the *right* children from the *right* families."

"And what's wrong with that? As a matter of fact, my wife and I had a get-together for Craig with a few of the kids who live in our neighborhood. He got along well with them. He was amazed with their school program with all the kinds of classes he hadn't been exposed to in public school. You certainly wouldn't have to worry with all that unnecessary taunting and crudeness he has to deal with daily."

"I thought Craig was going to get to know your family. Yet all along you had an agenda. I admit Craig has had a few problems, but no more than you and I did when we attended public school. The middle school is a good one, and I'm involved with his teachers and his school activities. On some level I think a public education can work for him. He has a chance to be exposed to kids from all kinds of backgrounds. He'll be a much better person and not some kid who is snotty and thinks he is better than anyone else."

Trey shrugged. "You should know Craig is receptive to the idea of living with me. He's crazy about his brothers and has already asked to return while he's on Christmas vacation from school."

"I have no problem with him visiting you, but I'm going to have to think long and hard on this private school deal and his living with you."

Trey stood. He grabbed his coat and called out to Craig, who quickly appeared in the doorway, munching on a sandwich. "Yeah, Dad, you still want a drink? I forgot. I was watching the television in the kitchen."

"No, I'm leaving. I've got to hit the road. Come give me a hug."

Craig walked up to his father, and they embraced quickly, the way men did.

"I'll be calling you before the week is out. Your mother said you could visit during your Christmas break. I've got to go."

"Don't forget the pictures of me and the twins."

"I'll e-mail them sometime tomorrow." Trey looked at Sasha. "Thanks for letting him come. You and I will talk more, when we're calmer and you're more rational." He gave her a frozen smile.

"Whatever, Trey." Sasha took hold of Craig's shoulders as they walked his father to the door. "Have a safe trip."

"Thank you. You two have a good week."

It took everything in Sasha to keep from acting like a fool and slamming the door. She maintained her cool for the sake of Craig. What was going on was between her and Trey, and she wasn't going to drag Craig into it. She didn't want him to feel as though he had to take sides.

Once they were alone, Sasha told Craig, "It would be a good idea for you to take your luggage into the room and unpack. Be sure to put your dirty laundry in the hamper for me to wash later."

"Mom, Dad has a three-story house. I had a large room with my own bathroom. My bedroom had a sweet plasma television, and I even had an Xbox there. I met some new friends. The girls there are hot and smart."

Listening with interest, Sasha smiled. "I'm glad you had a good time, son. Now get that stuff out of here. I have a few chores to take care of. We have to get ready for the beginning of the week."

She watched him drag his luggage as though it weighed more than it did.

Sasha headed into the kitchen to wash the dishes she'd left there and clear the mess her son had made in the short time he'd been home. She couldn't stop thinking about Trey's suggestion. She was sure her grandmother would be upset by it. Sighing, Sasha longed for the comfort of Eric's presence, his interest and advice, and the ready encouragement he always had. In the meantime, she had decided she wasn't going to lay her situation on Eric when she heard from him. Eric had enough to deal with. After he had gotten his family issues resolved, she might share her problem with him. But why should she burden him? She had always had to deal with stuff like this on her own. True, she cared for him, but it was too soon to bring him into her family issues. She and he had barely gotten to know each other. She wanted to keep that romantic aura they had going for now. She liked the comfort zone she shared with his affection. It felt right for the moment.

Chapter 15

The Monday morning while Sasha was preparing for work, she had several concerns bothering her. The main one was the conversation she and Trey had had over Craig living with him. The other was Eric, who hadn't called her the night before like she expected. She decided she was going to call Eric to inquire after his father's health, and hopefully she could also learn in a matter-of-fact manner from Eric what that Gabrielle Ryan was up to as well.

The moment Craig left the house to catch the school bus, the house phone rang. Sasha's heart filled with excitement when she saw the caller ID. She answered the phone on the second ring. "Eric, I waited for your call last night."

"Good morning to you too," he said in a humorous tone.

"How are things there? Please tell me your father is better."

"He's progressing nicely. Thanks. How are you and Craig?"

"We're both fine. Craig just left for school. He had too much fun at his father's house."

"Too much fun?"

"Never mind that. We'll talk more about that another time. How are you?"

"I crashed last night. After I went to the hospital with my mother and Gabrielle, I came home and climbed into bed and didn't awake until this morning. I didn't know how tired I was until I hit the bed."

The mention of Gabrielle's name sent off waves of jealousy, but she didn't let on. "I'm glad you had a chance to get some rest. I was getting ready to return to work."

"I'm going to be out the rest of the week, I'm sure. I've already made arrangements to have someone cover for me with my patients and to do my deliveries. And I'm sure I can count on you to check with my patients as well."

"You don't even have to ask that. Is there anything else I can do for you?"

"There are some forms at the clinic that need to be taken care of. Can you check them out and make sure they get to the right places and people?"

"Consider it done."

"I'm missing you."

"I feel the same way." Sasha clutched the phone and smiled as though he could see her.

"By the way, I'm going to have to stand in for my father at his fraternity's event. They're having a charity ball, and my dad will be honored as man of the year with an award given to him. He and my mother had plans of attending, until his illness. I've volunteered to go in his place, and Gabrielle is going with me."

Sasha didn't like the idea of Gabrielle being his date, but she had no right to complain. She didn't want Eric to consider her petty. In fact, she was glad he'd told her firsthand, instead of her finding out later on.

"That's nice," she said softly. "An award like that can't go ignored. I'm sure your father is worthy and will be proud to have you accept it for him. And I'm sure Gabrielle is going to be pleased to be your date."

"Gabrielle and I are friends. She is a family friend. I don't want you to feel that I'm trying to hook up with her or anything like that."

"I trust you. It's Gabrielle I'm concerned about. I have a feeling she would like to have one more chance in your life."

"Sasha, you don't have anything to worry about. Haven't I told you I'm not interested in anyone but you? I thought you and I had bonded and I won your trust."

She sighed. "I'm trying to have faith in you. Gabrielle Ryan is a beautiful, sophisticated woman and a physician. Before I was formally introduced to her at the reception, I overheard her raving about you and the relationship you two had when you were in high school. I got the impression from overhearing her conversation with her girlfriend that she had come on a mission to get with you."

"Oh, really?" Eric said with a hint of amusement. "Gabrielle and I had our turn. I respect her and I like her, but there's no way she and I can be the way we were. All of that stuff happened when we were naïve kids."

"You're only human. Believe me, I know from experience how a woman can work her way into a man's life and turn his whole world upside down. A man can get caught up so easily." Sasha knew she should have let the subject go, but her insecurities got the better of her.

"Are you trying to get rid of me? It sounds as though you're looking for me to do something that will show you I'm not real with you or that I can't be the right man for you," Eric said, sounding slightly annoyed.

"It's not that. It's just that I don't want to be hurt like I've been in the past. My ex was always working with this woman physician and she always had to travel away to certain medical events whenever he had to. My husband denied there was ever anything going on. And then one day he came home and told me he wanted out of our marriage because he had fallen in love with that doctor, who had always been 'only a colleague' whenever I questioned their relationship."

"I'm sorry you had to go through that. But that was *your* ex. I'm not the same man he is. Please don't compare me to him. You've got to believe in me and trust me. If you don't, I'll feel as though I'm wasting my time trying to win your love."

Sasha hated the turn the conversation had taken and didn't mean to come off as possessive. "I'm not trying to get rid of you. I want to trust you."

"That settles it, then. This event that I'm attending with Gabrielle is no big deal. My mother thought it would be good for the two of us to get out. She wanted to show her gratitude to Gabrielle for being a comfort to her. Mom didn't let Ashley know how worried she was over my father. She wanted her to go on her honeymoon. And my father is improving every day."

"That's wonderful. It's the most important thing, to know that he is getting stronger."

"It is. Tell Craig hello for me. I will call tomorrow night when I believe you're settled and in bed. Maybe we can have a sexier conversation."

His words brought a smile that eased her anxiety. "Oh, I'll be looking forward to that conversation."

Before he hung up, Sasha heard a woman talking in the background.

"Eric, I'm ready whenever you are," the woman said.

Sasha knew Gabrielle was plotting to be alone with Eric.

"I'll be ready to go shortly," Eric said.

It took everything in Sasha not to make an issue out of the situation.

"Sasha, I'll get with you tomorrow. I've promised to drive Gabrielle to the Tyson Corner Mall."

"Oh, really?" Sasha said flatly.

"It's not that big of a deal. I'm only showing her some courtesy. She is a houseguest and a friend of the family."

"Whatever, Eric. I have to get ready to go to work. Like you said, we'll talk more tomorrow."

"Have a great day."

"I would tell you the same thing, but I'm sure Gabrielle will see to that."

"Don't be that way. It's not that serious."

"I'm no way. I understand you're under a lot of stress. Gabrielle is doing her best to make sure you and your mother keep busy. Why would I make a big deal over that? I'm not that selfish."

"I sure want to believe that. I want to believe you trust me."

"Oh, I trust you. Listen, I really have to go. Talk with you tomorrow. Bye-bye."

Sasha grabbed her things and left her apartment for work. She trusted Eric, but she had no trust for Gabrielle, not knowing what kind of tricks she would pull to lure Eric to her.

* * *

That day when Sasha returned to work from her weekend, the ward was extremely busy. In fact, things were so busy that she didn't have time to share all the excitement of her trip with Pam until they had lunch in the cafeteria that afternoon.

Settling in at a table with their trays, Pam said to Sasha, "At last, I can get an update on this fabulous society wedding I heard about."

"It was beautiful. The whole weekend was one big roller coaster of emotions for Eric's family, though. One minute, they were celebrating, and the next moment Mr. Prince collapsed with cardiac arrest."

Taking a bite of her food, Pam looked concerned. "I was sorry to hear that. When I learned Dr. Prince wouldn't be in for a couple weeks because of his father's illness, I was really surprised. I couldn't believe all of that had taken place."

"According to Eric, his father is a workaholic. Along with all the wedding activities, the guests, I suppose it only brought everything to a head with his health. I can imagine that Mr. Prince has probably been feeling bad but ignored his condition and considered it minor stress and fatigue. But Eric told me this morning, he's had his heart bypass surgery and is getting better."

"That's good to hear, but you know what I'm interested in. What went down between you and Eric before the medical drama? You two had time to get cozy in the hotel room he reserved for you." She took another bite of her food.

Sasha considered sharing her secrets with Pam. She sure didn't want her business with Eric all over the hospital.

"You can trust me, Sasha. Really, you can. I know I run my mouth about other folks' business, but I wouldn't do you like that. I like you, and I'd like to think you and I have become friends since you've come to Hope Hospital."

Pam had been kind to her. She had been one of the first people at the hospital to make her feel at ease and not like the new kid on the block. Pam always made a point of sharing a joke or cueing her in on who was dependable, who to watch her back around.

Sasha smiled. "I'm not going into details with you, but I will say Eric and I became more than friends."

Pam gushed, "You two are so perfect for each other. I'm so glad he's not wasting himself on any more skanks. Since he's taken time to get to know you, I've watched him turn into the good guy I always knew he really was. I've got to say he had his share of women who were more than willing to go through that player phase of his."

Sasha had begun to eat her salad, listening to Pam.

Pam leaned close to Sasha. "He really knows what to do, doesn't he?"

"Pam!" Sasha's face turned a rosy pink.

"This is between the two of us, girl. I'm not

asking for details. I just want to know, is he a decent lover?"

"You've seen his smooth swagger and what great hands the man has." Sasha grunted softly. "The man definitely knows how to please. I'm not giving up any more info."

"You've said enough. I'm happy for you. Fine, rich, and satisfying, Dr. Prince is the complete package. I only hope this thing between the two of you gets better and better. After what you shared with me about your first marriage and heartache, you're certainly way overdue for a decent man in your life."

"It's good to have someone to talk about this with. I do like Eric. But I got an unexpected surprise at the wedding."

"What's that?"

"Eric's first girlfriend attended the wedding. Her name is Dr. Gabrielle Ryan; she's an internist."

"Wow! They go way back. I mean, I've seen them playing hanky-panky, but I didn't know they had a relationship. Anyway, go ahead. Tell me what happened."

"Well, during the reception, Mrs. Prince introduced her to me as the daughter of their best friends, and Eric's first love. Mrs. Prince shared with everyone at the table how pleased she and Gabrielle's mother were that their kids had a romance. Mrs. Prince said she and Mrs. Ryan were hoping that Eric and Gabrielle would have a relationship that would last until they had started their medical careers. They'd wanted them to be married, so they all could be one big happy family."

"Yuk! Hearing something like that would have made me feel uncomfortable."

"Oh, my confidence was shaken. Then Mrs. Prince insisted Gabrielle take a picture with her family. She didn't invite me in the picture."

"No! I would have been offended." Pam scowled. "You did get pictures with Eric, though, right?"

"Unfortunately, there was no time to do so. Right after they had their little picture-taking session with Gabrielle, Eric's father collapsed and there was nothing but confusion." Sasha's face revealed her remorse as she took another bite of her food.

"Oh, girl, I'm sorry. So the presence of this woman sort of took the spotlight off you and Eric. That's a shame."

"You haven't heard the worst of it yet. I left Gabrielle with Eric, so to speak. Being she is a family friend and his sister went away with her husband for her honeymoon, Gabrielle insisted on staying at Mrs. Prince's house to give moral support. Dr. Ryan claimed she had taken a few weeks off to rest and rejuvenate herself from working so hard."

"Oh, hell no. So what you're telling me is that Eric and this woman who was his first love are staying under the same roof."

"Exactly. And what makes it so bad, Pam, is the

fact that I overheard Gabrielle speaking with a friend of hers and telling her how she would love to have another chance with Eric. It seems the only reason they broke up was that after high school they went to colleges far away from each other. Their long-distance relationship couldn't withstand the other interests they developed while apart."

"Are you worried? I know I would be suspicious. There's nothing worse than a woman scheming to get into a man's heart to share his life."

"Tell me about it. I've already lived that whole experience with my ex."

"Let's not think negatively. I'm willing to give him the benefit of the doubt. I believe the man is excited over what he's found with you."

"I want to believe that too. I also know that sometimes it doesn't take much for a man to have a change of heart. While I was getting to know his mother, I didn't hide the fact that I had a teenage son. She was surprised by my revelation and quickly calculated that I'd been a teen mother. You should have seen the way she looked at me. Her expression let me know that I hadn't made a positive point with her standards."

"Oh no, she didn't. What's the big deal about that? You did get married and took responsibility for raising your child."

"Evidently, the people who live in the Princes' world all do things according to a certain plan. I know whenever Mrs. Prince looks at me she will probably think of me as urban or hip-hop trash."

"You can't worry about what she thinks. As long as Eric is pleased with the woman you've become, that's all that really matters."

"That's what I keep telling myself. I'm hoping that, once she gets a chance to know me, she will only focus on who I have become and not stereotype me as a loser or a young girl who grew up too fast."

"Don't waste your energy on Mrs. Prince and your initial meeting. I'm sure she'll see you differently when she understands how much Eric cares."

Sasha smiled at her friend's words of encouragement.

"Listen, I've got something I've got to share with you," Pam said. "Mia Evans was on the floor this weekend while I worked. She let me know she had seen you and Eric in the cafeteria and she could see how into each other you two were. She tried to get me to talk about you and him, but I didn't offer up anything. She claims she remembers you from your old neighborhood and that you two attended the same high school."

"I thought she looked familiar. I believe she's a few years younger than I am. I'm pretty sure she's familiar with my humiliating family situation from those days."

Pam gave her a questioning look.

"Since you're my friend, I'll tell you something about me I don't like known. Anyway, when I was growing up, my mother was a serious drug addict, and because she wasn't capable of taking care of me, my grandparents raised me. Back in those days my mother was a shameful mess, always hanging out with other druggies, getting high and doing whatever to get money for a fix. In fact she was often arrested for shoplifting. In school the kids teased me and made me feel like trash every chance they could. My grandmother and grandfather did their best to help keep her straight, but they fought a losing battle. My mother ended up overdosing and was found dead on a street with a needle still in her arm."

"Oh my goodness," Pam said, looking sympathetic. "I'm so sorry to hear that."

"My life was a living hell with her and without her. As a child, I blamed myself for her condition. Then I went through a stage where I was angry because she wouldn't get herself together, so she could be with me and be a regular mom, loving me. Now you can understand how I fell for the first guy who showed me attention and gave me affection. As a teen, I craved a normal relationship and a family. I was naïve to believe I could show everyone who made fun of me that I wasn't like my mother. I'm sure the me Mia remembers are all those unpleasant things I want to forget."

"Mia Evans was in love with Eric. Remember, she was one of his bed partners before he decided to get his life together. Mia has been giving me a bad vibe. I think she is jealous of you. I heard she's been going through some changes ever since Eric dropped her cold."

Sasha shrugged. "Should I have to watch my back because of her?" She smiled wryly.

"I have a feeling she is hurt by Eric. I think she actually believed she was going to get him to be her man, but everyone knows she was just another booty call for Eric at the time. You might get some dirty looks or a cold shoulder, you know, that immature stuff losers pull."

Sasha shook her head. All she knew was she didn't want any trouble. She was taking care of her business and sure didn't want anyone interfering in her living her life. Just as they were finishing their lunch, Pam got a page to report to her desk in the ward.

"I can't even eat my lunch in peace. I bet that's the lab technician I've been trying to get in touch with for most of the morning. They've hired this new person who is a big whiner and is always late sending out reports." Pam stood and cleared away her trash. "I might as well clock back in. I only have a few minutes left anyway. See you upstairs," she said, hustling away.

Glancing at her watch, Sasha realized she only had ten minutes left on her lunch herself. Since she had eaten her food, she began fanning through a magazine she'd brought along. Suddenly, a tray was slid onto her table. She looked up and saw Mia Evans giving her a frozen smile.

"I hope you don't mind me sitting here," Mia said, taking a seat.

"No. I was getting ready to leave anyway." Sasha noticed that there were other tables where Mia could have sat. She sensed that Mia had a purpose for joining her.

Mia stared at Sasha. "It's funny how we both work here and haven't had the chance to talk. Do you remember me from high school?"

"How can I not? Although I was a senior when you were a sophomore, I do remember you being quite popular. Let's see, you were Miss Sophomore, and you were a cheerleader as well. Isn't that right?"

Mia's eyes widened. "All of that is true." She laughed nervously. "You were the girl everyone was talking about who had gotten pregnant by her college boyfriend. And you had a mother who was a shameless junkie."

Glowering at her, Sasha bolted out of her seat to leave.

Mia took hold of her arm and stared at her wildly. "Don't rush off. I'm only telling the truth. There's no need for you to get offended." A wicked smiled eased the corners of her mouth.

Sasha snatched her arm out of the woman's grip. "I don't have to listen to this. Who do you think you are?"

"I was Eric's woman until you came along. How dare you ruin what I had with him."

Troubled by this woman's tone and her

accusation, Sasha turned and walked away from the table. She heard Mia's chair fall to the floor and glanced back, only to see Mia following her toward the exit and outside into the hallway.

"Sasha! Wait!"

Feeling the crazed woman on her heels, Sasha whirled around quickly because she didn't trust what Mia might do, and backed away from her slightly.

"Leave Eric Prince alone," Mia warned through gritted teeth, her tone full of venom. "I mean that. If you don't, I will make your life a living hell."

Without saying a word, Sasha hurried off and reached the elevator, which was loading with visitors and employees, and climbed on. As the doors slid shut, she noticed that Mia stood watching her as though she were prey.

Chapter 16

"This affair reminds me of the way you and I used to make the rounds to all those teen formals," Gabrielle said to Eric while they danced slowly.

"You really still think about those things?"

"Of course I do. That time will always be special to me. You were my first love, Eric." She tossed her long caramel-colored hair over her shoulder and lavished a teasing smile on him.

"Let's not do memory lane. Let's leave it in the past where it belongs."

Gabrielle poked out her bottom lip, feigning hurt. "How can you be such a grouch?"

"I just want to relax and enjoy myself."

"You have every right to relax and enjoy yourself. Your father is recovering wonderfully and will be released from the hospital on the weekend." She placed her hand on the side of his face and leveled it with hers. "I want you to act like you want to be with me. If you don't show me a good time, I'm going to tell your mother," she teased.

Eric wasn't in the mood for this dance. He had accepted the award for his father and had made the rounds to friends of the family and to his father's fraternity brothers to let them know how well his father was progressing, thanking those who had made calls and sent gifts to cheer his dad. If Gabrielle hadn't volunteered to tag along with him, he would have slipped away quietly, but his mother had insisted that they stay and have fun. She was anxious to show Gabrielle how much she appreciated her support and all the errands she had helped her with during Ashley's absence.

At the end of the dance, Eric escorted Gabrielle to the bar and ordered drinks. He wanted one badly. He'd spoken with Sasha earlier and she was rather cool with him. When he questioned her, she merely told him she had some things on her mind that had been troubling her but refused to tell what they were. He knew she was only being considerate of him and what he was dealing with in his family. Or was she upset because he would be having a night out with Gabrielle?

"Tell me something about that woman you brought to the wedding as your date." Garielle sipped on her white wine. "Did you know your mother is concerned that you may have lowered your standards in women? She told me this woman has a teen son and believes that she may have loose morals."

It angered Eric to know his mother had been

sharing his personal life with Gabrielle. He was pretty sure that Gabrielle, taking advantage of how much his mother admired her, didn't have a difficult time prying the info out of her. His mother still thought of Gabrielle as that outgoing girl who was the prettiest and brightest young woman in their social circle and hadn't noticed that she had grown into an arrogant woman. Gabrielle was an attractive woman, but she was consumed by her career. At her age, she was probably ready to settle down and have a family, yet she had made medicine her priority for so long, she'd forgotten to think about her needs as a woman. From the conversations he and she had shared, Eric knew that Gabrielle had high standards when it came to the kind of men she would date. She had even admitted with bittersweet humor that, at her age, she didn't have much to choose from.

"Mom didn't have time to get to know Sasha, so she had no right to make any judgments concerning her character. Sasha is a great person and a hardworking mother who has managed to raise a decent son nearly on her own. By the way, her name is Sasha Michaels and not *that woman*. She is an outstanding registered nurse supervisor."

"Oh my goodness. You are really serious, aren't you? How gallant you are to come to her defense."

Eric took a sip of his Hennessy, his thoughts far off.

Gabrielle leaned on the bar in a seductive manner and eyed him. "Is her background the same as ours? Would she feel comfortable in our social circle? I can imagine on a one-to-one basis she is probably satisfying to you," she said cattily. "I observed her when she was at the reception. I could tell by the strained polite expression on her face that she was like a fish out of water around our kind."

"The more you talk, the more you show me how uncompassionate you are. You have become a snob. I thought you and I had always said we wouldn't be like our parents, who always wanted to shelter us from other people in our community. What happened to that young woman who used to make friends with anyone as long as they were civil to you?"

Gabrielle gave him an accusing stare. "We grew up privileged, Eric. Our parents wanted us to be professionals and to mate and have children as cultured and bright as we turned out."

"All of that is true, but I'm thankful I can think for myself. Being in medicine and working with all kinds of people, I've learned to be more empathetic. As far as I'm concerned, I'm no better than anyone else. All of us are human, with the same needs and desires."

She pursed her lips in distaste. "You're so idealistic. You're setting yourself up for heartache again." She sipped her wine. "You know for yourself how upset our families get when they feel we've crossed the boundaries. When I was in college I remember my parents had a fit when they learned I was dating a football player from a working-class family. The moment that semester ended, before the summer even began, my parents sent me away to Europe with some other girls I had been in Jack and Jill with. Some kind of way the parents had managed to find a work-study program for us in Paris, so we could expand our résumés."

Eric knew how strict all of their parents had been. A lot of them were hypocrites. One minute they were working on committees to reach out to and mentor inner-city kids, to improve their experiences and to emphasize the importance of education. The next, they spoke about how bad of an influence those kids were and how they didn't want their children socializing with the generation they referred to as the hip-hoppers who did nothing but fill people's minds with negative images of cultured and educated African-Americans.

"I can't believe you. You refuse to live your life out of your parents' shadow. True, while we were growing up, there was stress on us to live a certain way and to socialize with certain people. Life has taught me that selfishness and arrogance have no place in medicine or even in my personal life. Gabrielle, it is so easy to simply live and take your happiness whenever you can." He tossed back the last of his drink. "I'm ready to go," he announced coldly.

Staring at him, Gabrielle was bothered that their conversation had grown so heated. She had to set things right with him. Her night wasn't turning out the way she had intended. Hearing the band play a lovely ballad, she took Eric's hand.

"The last thing I wanted to do was to get on

your bad side. I came with you for support and to see some old friends our families have in common. I had no idea we'd end up in a heated conversation over that woman—excuse me, Sasha Michaels. Although we may differ, we'll still be friends, right?"

Eric shrugged. "You have a right to your opinions."

She smiled. "Let's share this dance together. I don't know when I'll get a chance like this again."

Eric gave her a stony look.

"Please. You used to like to dance with me. We've known each other too long to let a conversation like this come between us."

Smiling reluctantly, he led her onto the dance floor and swung her into his arms to fall into the rhythm of the song.

As they swayed to the music, Gabrielle turned up her charm. "Well, I'll be out of your hair after tomorrow. I'm going to New York to visit some friends, catch a couple shows, and check out the nightlife there."

"Mom is going to miss you. You've really been a comfort to her."

"It was no problem at all. From the time you and I were a couple, I've always felt like a part of your family. Will you miss me too, Eric Prince?"

"This has been an extremely stressful week. It's been good to have you here with us. I've seen firsthand how one crisis can turn a family upside down. Yes, I will miss having you around. You've become like family to me."

"I certainly didn't want to hear that 'family' part coming from you. I have to confess, staying in the house with you has made me remember all the reasons why I was completely gone over you as a girl. Though you and I are older, I've noticed that you have seasoned quite well. You're more handsome, and that special charm you own has gotten stronger than ever."

"Are you flirting with me, Gabrielle?"

She laughed. "Flirting? I've lusted for you in my heart from the moment I saw you standing in front of the church as part of your sister's bridal party."

"If I didn't know better, I'd say you're coming on to me."

"I am. I was hoping you and I could share one night, if only for old times' sake and—"

"Whoa! I don't think that—"

"Shh!" Gabrielle laid a manicured finger over his lips. "I'm not looking for a commitment. I'm only looking for a night of passion, nothing more. I've already reserved a room in this hotel." She tossed her hair and gave him a daring look.

Had Gabrielle propositioned Eric before he had fallen for Sasha, he could easily have taken her on for the hell of it. But he had won Sasha's trust and didn't want to jeopardize that. Then he considered how much Gabrielle had changed. He sure didn't want her coming along later and making it known when he hoped to be happy with Sasha. Gabrielle was getting him all twisted mentally and physically. *This shouldn't be such a struggle*, he chided himself.

"I can't believe you have to think about my offer. I was hoping we could spend the night and forget our real lives."

Eric stopped dancing and stared deep into her eyes.

"You can trust me, hon. I won't ever tell a soul." She brushed her body against his and kissed his lips tenderly, holding his gaze.

At the touch of her lips, Eric closed his and tried to fight the power of his responding flesh. The heady scent of her perfume and the feel of her body aroused him. Cursing himself silently for his weakness he decided it'd be best to take her home before doing something he would later regret. He slipped an arm around her waist and led her toward the exit of the hotel ballroom.

It was Friday afternoon, and Sasha was feeling down when she went to visit her grandmother after work. Craig would be there waiting for her, because he had gotten out of school early that day. She had a thumping headache from everything swirling around in her mind.

Ever since Mia had threatened her, she was constantly watching her back. She had made up her mind that she was going to report her to security if she said or did anything out of the way. Sasha thought the woman was delusional and really didn't have any business working at this time. She'd checked with other nurses who had worked with her, and they hadn't seen the dark side Mia had shown her. In fact, they claimed that she was capable as always.

Somewhat relieved it was only a personal issue, Sasha kept her peace. She hoped Mia would be able to pull herself together and not have any more of the meltdowns she had had with her.

Next to plague her mind was the issue of Eric and Gabrielle attending this charity dance on his father's behalf. Whenever she spoke to Eric during their nightly conversations, Gabrielle always managed to be somewhere near him, making her presence known.

Sasha remembered her husband had cheated on her and then left her to marry his present wife. Eric and she hadn't been together for long, so she knew he could walk out of her life if he chose. She knew Gabrielle Ryan was taking advantage of the situation, and could just imagine them spending evenings reminiscing over their past romance, which could be easily rekindled with a simple gesture or the right phrase.

To top everything else, Sasha feared losing custody of her son to Trey. How fair was that? Ever since Craig had returned from his visit with Trey, every evening he mentioned what a big house his father had, that he had his own room that Trey's wife told him he could decorate and call his. Of course, he had fallen for his twin brothers and wanted to be with them as much as Sasha would allow.

Inside her grandmother's house, she was

greeted by the comforting aroma of Grandma Claudia's baking. Sasha called out, "Hello!"

Craig popped out of the living room and greeted her in the hall as she removed her coat and hung it in the closet. He hovered near her.

"Mom, I talked to Dad a little while ago," Craig said, leaning against the wall. "He wants me to come for another visit on the weekend after Christmas. He wants me to spend New Year's Day with them."

Sasha frowned. "You haven't even asked me how I am before you get to telling me about what your father wants me to do."

Craig stood upright. "I'm sorry. How are you, Mom?"

"I'm okay," she said curtly. Then she observed his puzzled expression and felt guilty for being short with him.

Craig trailed her as she walked toward the kitchen. "I'm supposed to call Dad later. What do I tell him?"

Sasha whirled toward her son. "Let me get settled for a minute, Craig. We'll talk about all this after I've had a chance to spend some time with Grandma."

"A'ight." He headed back to the living room, where music videos played.

Grandma Claudia greeted Sasha with her usual warmth. "Hi, lady. How are you today?"

"I wish I could be 'a'ight' like Craig," she said, chuckling, "but I'm aiming to be that way."

"Still struggling with those ideas Trey has gotten that boy all excited over, huh?"

"Am I being selfish for not wanting Craig to leave me?" Sasha sat down to eat the cookies her grandmother had made for a bake sale the following day.

"No, dear. That's your baby, no matter how old he is. It's been the two of you for quite a while. You're right to think on this situation until you feel right about it."

"Who would ever think Trey would want to breeze into our lives and make an offer to send Craig to a private school and even want him to be with his new family?" Sasha said, moving to the refrigerator for milk.

"I know it doesn't seem fair, but that's the way some men operate. A woman has to hang in with the kids through all the bad times and good times. She often has to let her needs go for her child's sake. A man can walk away and have the freedom to do whatever he wants, yet when he sees the light and sees how great that child is turning out, most of the time he wants to step in and be proud of what you have molded. If a woman stands in the way of allowing a man to know his child, it's considered wrong. I had a feeling Trey would come around. You've got a fine young man in Craig. Trey would be crazy if he didn't want him in his life or those babies' lives."

"Life is so frustrating. Just when you have everything together, it throws you a curve that knocks you right on your behind." Sasha grabbed another cookie.

Her grandmother stared at her, peeping over the glasses perched on her nose. "What's up with you and Eric? I know you told me his father had gotten better. So when is he returning to town?"

"I was hoping one day next week. I talked with him late last night. His mother has hired a male nurse to come help her when his father comes home."

"I'm glad to hear Eric's father is better. But you still didn't answer my question. How are you and Eric making out as a couple? I do know you care for him. It's written all over your face. That man has a way of making you glow. People who saw the two of you at church that Sunday remarked how perfect the two of you looked together. Some of the busybodies even told me I'd better get ready for a wedding." Grandma Claudia's eyes twinkled with mischief.

Sasha was amused. "I was wondering when I was going to hear about the speculations. Those sisters don't miss anything. I can't give you an answer, other than I do like Eric a lot. He's involved in something and someone this evening that I'm skeptical of."

"Really?" Grandma Claudia spooned the last of the cookie dough onto the tray and placed it in the oven. "What's he doing, baby?"

"While I was at the wedding, Eric's old high school flame showed up. She's a physician too. When his father took sick, she invited herself to stay at his family home right where Eric is staying. According to Mr. and Mrs. Prince, Gabrielle is considered like family. After watching her around Eric during the reception, I have this gut feeling she'd like to rekindle the romance they had."

A concerned-looking Grandma Claudia grunted. "Maybe you're overreacting."

"How would you feel if you knew your man was taking another woman to a formal charity event this evening? You see, Eric's father is being honored as man of the year. Due to his illness, Eric volunteered to attend, and his ex-girl made herself his date."

Her grandmother dropped down on a chair and removed her eyeglasses and rubbed her eyes. "I wouldn't trust a woman like that around a man of mine. That's for sure. But you're going to have to give him the benefit of the doubt on this one. This whole situation could show exactly what kind of man he'll be with you."

Sasha knew there was truth in her grandmother's words. What if she found out that Eric hadn't become the man he had been trying to convince her he was—trustworthy and devoted?

Chapter 17

Sasha was troubled by the fact that Eric hadn't called her that Friday evening after he'd attended the charity event with Gabrielle. Though curious as to how the function had been with Gabrielle as his supposedly fake date, she was determined not to call him. All kinds of thoughts went through her mind. She imagined Gabrielle made sure that Eric took notice of her and reminded him of what they once meant to each other. Could Eric have fallen prey to Gabrielle's wiles?

Sasha wanted him for herself and didn't want to think of him in that woman's arms or kissing her lips. She had missed him so much in the last few days, her body ached for his touch, and her eyes hungered to see his wonderful, handsome face with that sparkle in his eyes she felt he had only for her. Christmas was only a few days away, and she didn't want to be without Eric at her side.

Sasha was glad she had an evening shift at the Free Clinic that Saturday. There she knew she could drown herself in her work. Hopefully, Eric would call her there to assure her everything was still intact for them as a couple.

Just as Sasha expected, it was relatively busy with older patients complaining of symptoms of colds—fevers, hard coughs, aches and pains in their joints. Others were dealing with holiday stress that had sent their blood pressure and glucose levels soaring.

Dr. Porter was standing in for Eric that evening. A lot of the patients were disappointed that the kindhearted Dr. Prince wasn't available. The instant they learned of his family emergency, they all wanted to make sure Sasha sent their regards to him. To Sasha, the patients' admiration of Eric was a testament to the marvelous physician and man he was.

As Sasha entered the exam room, Mrs. Preston, a regular senior patient, asked, "Honey, when my boy be back?"

Wrapping the blood pressure cup around her arm, Sasha said, "We're looking for him to return sometime next week."

Mrs. Preston stared at Sasha. "Can this Dr. Porter take care of me as well as Dr. Prince? I look forward to seeing that one. He always takes time to answer all my questions without getting impatient with me. He's special, that Dr. Prince." She covered her mouth with tissues as she went into a bout of coughing and sneezing.

"Well, you certainly can't wait for Dr. Prince to return." Sasha smiled. "Dr. Porter will have you a lot better." She recorded the vital signs on her chart and gave her a comforting squeeze on her shoulder.

"Sweetie, Dr. Prince told me he was single. And I don't see any wedding rings on your hand."

Sasha blushed. "Mrs. Preston, are you trying to play matchmaker?"

With a flash of joy in her watery eyes, Mrs. Preston said, "Ah . . . I see that color in your face. I'm not too old to know what that means." She chuckled. "You two young people would make a real nice couple. Whenever you're around him, I've caught his eyes shining too."

"Mrs. Preston, you are too much. I have to agree with you, though. He is an extraordinary doctor and a gentleman."

"Take my advice and grab that man, daughter. You hear? I understand a good man is hard to find these days."

Amused, Sasha said, "I will take your words under consideration." She closed the lady's chart and slipped it inside the pocket outside the door. "Dr. Porter will be in shortly." Sasha left and eyed her watch, wondering what Eric was doing at this moment.

* * *

It was a little after nine o'clock that evening by the time Sasha locked the door on the clinic. Just as she had flipped the open sign to closed, she was consumed with joy and excitement at seeing Eric striding toward her. As he stepped onto the well-lit sidewalk, he looked as though he had been heaven-sent to her. Her heart raced, and her arms ached to hold him. She snatched open the door and leaped into his arms to greet him.

Enfolding her in his arms, Eric kissed her hard and long. He pressed his face into her buttery complexion. "I've missed you so much," he whispered in her ear.

"One more day without seeing you would have driven me crazy." Sasha rested her head on his chest and could hear his heart beating as fast as hers.

Coming out of the fog of their reunion, she took him by the hand and led him inside from the cold night and locked the door behind them. She gazed up at him and held on to his hand. "I assume your father is better."

"He came home today. My mother hired a nurse to help her care for him. She encouraged me to return here. I believe she wanted me out of the house, so she could be alone with my dad and spoil him. And she knew I had business to take care of in my office and at the hospital. I made a stop at Hope Hospital and checked on some things there before heading here."

"What about Gabrielle? Is she still there with your mother?"

Eric's facial expression dimmed. "Uh, she's gone too. She left this afternoon. She had plans with friends in New York."

"I was worried when I didn't hear from you last night. I imagined her seducing you and—"

Dr. Porter came out of his office, wearing his overcoat. "Hey, there's the big guy. Good to have you back, buddy. How's your father?"

"He's doing much better, thank you. He came home this morning."

"Great!" Dr. Porter exclaimed. "I did my best to hold down things here in your absence. Nurse Michaels helped me to make it seem as though you were running this place."

Eric beamed at her. "What can I say? She's one of the best in her profession. That's why she's working here."

"I can't argue with you on that point. Well, since you're here, I'm leaving. Will you make sure Sasha gets safely to her car? I have to go to the hospital to check on a few patients there."

"Go on. I'll take care of her. I stopped by to check on my mail and e-mail, so I'll be here awhile. You don't mind waiting with me, do you, Sasha?" Eric stared at her with amusement.

"Of course not. I have to restock some of the exam rooms with supplies."

"In that case, I'll say good night. Be careful. You have to watch yourselves even more since the

Christmas holiday is approaching. With the way the economy is, people are a bit more desperate. A couple of nights ago, I understand, there were a couple of break-ins to some of the businesses, and then a couple of cars were robbed that had holiday shopping bags exposed inside the car. I think we should consider hiring security for these late evenings we spend here. Well, I'm leaving."

Sasha followed Dr. Porter to the door to see him out and to lock the door. Then she closed the vertical blinds from peering eyes. "Now we're alone." She hurried into Eric's arms and possessed his lips with a hungry passion.

He welcomed her hot kisses with ardent ones, and they became a tangle of groping hands and arms. The two of them made their way to the nearest hallway off the reception area. Leaning against the wall, he and she ground together and kissed until soft moans of delight came from them.

Eric shook off his leather jacket and let it fall to the floor. In a dance of urgent passion, he seized Sasha by her waist and took hold of her hand to tow her into his office, to the leather sofa, where he pulled her on top of him, kissing her and fondling her bottom.

Lost in his strong embrace and the sweetness of his kisses, she was grateful she was his woman now. Her heart swelled with such bliss, she knew right then and there she was in love. As Eric nibbled and licked on her earlobe, her body felt aflame. She assisted him as he tugged the top of her uniform up and over her head and then freed her breasts from her bra in a flash.

He buried his face between her luscious breasts as he sat upright to taste the tip of one perfect globe and then the other, sending shivers down her spine. Sasha was moist and ready.

Sasha gripped his shoulders and tilted her head back, to savor the raw fervor that sizzled through her veins. With him in between her thighs and his hardness pressed against her hot mound, she swayed her hips to the delicious tingle of pleasure. She palmed the sides of his face and plunged her tongue between his lips and inside his mouth. His ready tongue caressed hers.

Suddenly, Eric lifted her up and flipped her down on the sofa on her back. With an earnest grip he took hold of the waistband of her uniform and panties and removed them hastily.

Completely nude, Sasha lay there breathing heavily with anticipation. In the darkened room she could see his silhouette removing his clothes. Then she heard the ripping of a condom wrapper. Knowing of his preparations, she wished there was a light she could reach, so she could see every inch of his beautiful bronze body and every gorgeous erect inch of his sure-to-please shaft.

"Don't torture me any longer," she said in a husky, sensual tone, her body quivering with expectation.

Eric wasted no more time. He sat near her and sought her dewy, heated center, probing it briefly with his fingers, before sliding himself ever so slowly and deeply within her with a low groan of satisfaction.

Sasha clung to him with all her might and treasured every inch of him within her, thrusting sweetly, lifting her hips up and down in a rhythmic tempo. She grew bolder and hungrier for him, murmuring words of praise. Eric made her feel as though this were her first real sexual encounter. The kisses and caresses they exchanged along their lovers' journey made her eyes tear up as he electrified every fiber within her heart and soul, and she could no longer restrain herself.

She wrapped her legs around Eric's waist and began to purr and utter his name. Grabbing each other and tongue kissing, their bodies gyrated wildly together.

They hit their peaks together with shouts and growls of rapture. From there they were both washed in a downpour of cascading ecstasy that lifted their spirits and hearts to a mesmerizing spiritual level of unity. Her arms closed around him, his whole body shook, and she quivered as though she had been hit by a power surge.

Lying together, drenched in perspiration and breathing heavily on the leather sofa, they laughed softly from their pleasure as they cuddled and enjoyed the afterglow of their intimacy.

"Oh my goodness! That was so great. So hot," he said in a drowsy tone, kissing her along her neck and breasts.

"I've got to agree on that. I'm convinced I'm in love. I don't have any qualms about admitting it either. The way you loved me lets me know you're for real." She moved on his warm, cozy body. "This feels real and right. You're that man I thought no longer existed. I certainly wouldn't have been able to give myself to you like I did if you hadn't proved your worth to me in the time we've been in this whirlwind romance." She hooked the back of his neck and lowered her now swollen lips to him and shared a delicious openmouthed kiss.

Eric caressed her firm behind. "I can't believe I've gotten Sasha Michaels—Miss No Nonsense—to say she loves me. Are you sure, lady?" he teased.

"Of course, I am. I never say anything I don't mean. I love you, Eric Prince. I've heard of people falling in love quickly, but I always thought those people were irrational. But now I've become a believer in the power of love. I do know, with the right man, it can only take a moment."

"You've ruined everything."

Sasha placed her hands on the sofa and pushed herself up to hover above him. His words had troubled her. What could he mean? Then she remembered he hadn't finished telling her about Gabrielle and last night, but she wasn't going to bring it up. Obviously, Gabrielle was insignificant to him from the way he'd made love to her.

"Before you jump to the wrong conclusions, hear me out." Eric brushed her damp hair behind her ears. "After all the disappointments I've had with women, being with you is more than I ever dreamed. I wanted to be the one to say I love you first. And, hell, I thought I was going to have to climb a mountain to hear you tell me, 'I love you.' I had a bad reputation to live down. Once you smiled at me and I saw what a kind and sensitive woman you were, I knew you were the one for me. I had a little time to convince you I wasn't a philanderer. That wasn't who I really was. I had issues I was dealing with, and I chose an unreasonable way to get over my heartache and disappointment. I'm glad you came into my life. You woke me up and made me remember who I am. You've made me a better man, baby."

Falling back on the sofa, Sasha hugged Eric's nude body. She took his chin and turned his face to hers. "One more time. I have to have another go-around with you, knowing what we have is love and the chance at a meaningful relationship."

Eric rolled to her and held her. "Fine by me, my angel. Let me get another love glove. I want you to be the only baby in my life."

As he left her side briefly, Sasha laughed and spanked his behind.

The two of them made passionate love again, which was as sweet and memorable as the first time.

Afterward, they snuggled and napped until their energy returned. Then they dressed and made their way out of the clinic a little after 2:00 A.M. into the dark, cold winter morning.

As they strolled arm in arm and close together as though they were the only people in the world, Sasha told Eric that she didn't have to rush home since Craig was spending the evening with her grandmother to help her with chores that day.

"In that case, there's no reason why you can't come home with me. I'd love to wake up with you by my side. I don't want you out of my sight."

"That sounds perfect for me. I want to hold on to this feeling as much as you. I've got to get home before two in the afternoon, though. My grandmother is going to drop Craig off at home after they attend church."

"Oh, this situation is getting better all the time." He hugged her close to his side. Reaching Eric's car, Sasha and he leaned against it, embracing and kissing, when suddenly a gunshot rang out, hitting the rear window of Eric's car and shattering it. Eric held on to a screaming Sasha, and they dropped to a kneeling position, out of the range of gunfire.

"What's going on?" Sasha asked, her voice shaking with fear.

Eric whipped out his cell phone from his jacket and tried to call the police. Before he could complete his call, another shot rang out. This time the bullet hit the window right above where he and Sasha had squatted for safety.

"Damn it!" Eric eyed his surroundings while holding on to Sasha. He made another attempt at calling for help and got through.

Just then another shot hit the headlight of his car.

Sasha clung to him and said in a hushed tone, "This seems personal. Whoever is shooting is out to get one of us."

"Stay down. I'm going to try to communicate." Eric lifted his head cautiously and called out, "What is it that you want? If it's money, I can toss my wallet out on the parking lot."

There was no response.

Still, Eric reached in his slacks and pulled out his wallet and tossed it out on the lot. Then he saw a figure in a hood and jeans march out from behind a pillar of the sidewalk shopping center. The person kicked the wallet aside and came walking in the direction of Eric and Sasha, holding the gun as though ready to shoot again. "I need you to try to be as calm as possible. I'm going to confront this thug." Rising to his height, Eric jammed his hand in his jacket and pretended he had a firearm.

The assailant person dropped the hood.

Eric swore loudly when he realized it was Mia Evans.

"I saw you leaving the hospital tonight. How dare you leave me? You cheated on me and took her to meet your family. The whole hospital knows of the romance with that tramp that the two of you think no one knows about. Why do you have to disrespect me, Eric? I told everyone you loved me, wanted to marry me. Then you humiliate me by acting like a teenager with her. You went in the clinic early, and it's damn near morning and you two come out hugged up. When did the clinic turn into a Holiday Inn for screwing?"

Eric could see Mia's eyes were dazed and her face washed in tears as she stood near a streetlight.

"Hand me the gun, so no one will get hurt," Eric said calmly. "You're in a no-win situation. The police are on their way."

"I still love you. You treated me like a whore. How could you do that to me?" Mia said, her speech slurred as though she'd been drinking or using drugs. She held the gun with both hands and aimed it at Eric.

As two police cars rolled into the parking lot, Mia fired her weapon and hit Eric, who dropped to the ground beside Sasha, moaning in agony.

Sasha gasped, hovering over him. "Dear God, please don't let him leave me too. Eric! Eric!" In the darkness, she felt his body until she found where the blood was pouring from. She removed her neck scarf and placed pressure on the area to halt the flow.

Another bullet was fired, but Sasha wasn't fazed. She was too busy trying to revive Eric. Then she felt a stinging pain in her shoulder. With bloody hands, she grabbed it, and the next thing she knew, she was slipping into darkness, hearing only the shouts and orders of the police officers.

Chapter 18

Six months later

"Sasha, you look fabulous," Crystal said, fussing with the curls in the swept-away-from-the-face look she'd given her friend. "You've gotten your Prince. Yes, you have. That man is a Prince in more ways than one, you lucky lady."

"I'm sure I've got it right this go-round. I can't help but live a happily-ever-after life." Sasha laughed, her eyes sparkling, her heart full of joy.

"This is your day, and I'm going to let you talk about your man as much as you want for today. After today, I'm not going to want to hear my husband this and my husband that from you. I only want you to tell me your husband has a friend or colleague he wants to hook me up with, okay?"

"I hear you, Crystal. I'm going to look out for you." Sasha stared at what a beautiful job Crystal was doing with her hair for the wedding.

"You and Eric are due the happiness you've found."

"I know. Can you believe all the drama it took for us to have this day? Who would ever have thought Mia would carry things as far as she did, trying to wipe us out?"

"Temporary insanity is what her lawyer pleaded for her, but she still will be locked away for a while. I heard she had a complete breakdown. Someone mentioned to me in the shop that the hospital had learned she'd been swiping drugs from there for her use. She had become addicted to several painkillers and was also in a lot of debt. She'd lost her car and the town house she'd been living in for the last few years. And she blamed Eric for her problems. I bet she imagined he would marry her and end all her problems, with his wealth."

"Who will ever know what went on in her mind? All I can do is hope she gets herself together to begin her life again whenever she gets out. She can forget nursing or even working in this area again."

"How can you be so empathetic, Sasha, after what she did?"

Sasha shrugged, not wishing to talk about Mia anymore. She thought of the many problems her mother had had before she died. She knew there were people who didn't approve of her mother's lifestyle, yet they were always praying and hoping she would come through her horrible turmoil.

"Can we talk about something more pleasant?

The bride wants to only speak of happy things, so she can have pleasant thoughts and memories for today."

"Uh-oh, you're speaking in the third person. Are you turning into a 'bridezilla' on me?" Crystal laughed. "Here's a good subject to kick around. Are you and your man going to start having kids on your honeymoon?"

Amused, Sasha gazed up at Crystal. "Since you are my good friend, I will share this with you. Eric and I definitely want a child together. We've discussed it, and it's a priority for us right after we say our vows. We will have plenty of time to work on baby-making. Craig will be going to live with his father after the summer to attend that fancy private school he's been begging me to attend."

"I can't believe you're letting that boy out of your sight."

"That's why I'm letting him go. I've visited the school. It's something he can definitely benefit from. I want the best for him. He's a young man, and he needs a father at this point in his life. I can't do anything more than continue to love him. He'll be seeing me often. Craig is counting the days until he gets his driver's license. Can you believe that? His father has already promised him a car if he makes the dean's list."

Sasha's eyes grew misty, thinking about how grown-up her boy had become. Today, it didn't take much to make her teary-eyed. She was such a bundle of nerves. "And even though Eric and I will be moving into a new house, we've already set aside a room for Craig to call his very own."

"You and Eric have really planned this happily-ever-after thing."

"I can't say it enough. That man is simply wonderful."

Grandma Claudia came into the dressing room of the church, looking gorgeous in a bright yellow outfit. Crystal had taken care of her hair and makeup and turned her into a sassy-looking sixty-something woman for the day.

"How's my baby holding up?" Grandma Claudia placed her hands on Sasha's shoulders and eyed her in the oval mirror they shared.

"I'm fine, happy, and feeling blessed, Grandma. Eric is going to be my husband." Sasha whirled around in her strapless satin gown and embraced her.

As she returned the hug, her grandmother's eyes sparkled with tears. "You look beautiful. Just like a princess, my dear."

"I'm almost too much for myself today." Sasha laughed with delight. Seeing the tears in her grandma's eyes, she touched her face affectionately. "Are you thinking about my mom today too?"

"Oh, baby, yes. To be honest with you, there's not a day that goes by that I don't have a thought of her. I wish I could have saved her from herself. If only she could see . . ." Grandma Claudia lowered her head and wept softly. She pulled out a linen handkerchief from her purse and dabbed her eyes carefully. "I'd give anything for her to have been around to share this day with me, see the wonderful grandson she has."

Giving Sasha a sad look, she said, "Toward the end of her life, she tried to change her ways, but she wasn't strong enough to fight that addiction. I want you to know that." Through her sadness she forced a smile. She cleared her throat. "This is your day. Today is not a day for tears, unless they are tears of joy. Not only did I come in here to see you before you come down the aisle, but I have a surprise for you." She opened her purse. "I should have given it to you last night, but I had hidden it so well, I nearly didn't find it." She chuckled a bit.

Sasha wondered what her grandmother could have for her.

Grandma Claudia pulled out something wrapped in tissue paper and opened it carefully to reveal a white gold chain with a beautiful heart pendant.

"That's lovely. Have you been saving this for me for a long time?" Sasha asked, thinking it was a keepsake she had bought long ago for her.

"I have. But it's not from me. It's from your mother."

Looking puzzled, Sasha waited for an explanation.

"Why and when, right? Your mother gave this to me for you about a year before we lost her. It was during one of her many hopeful somber days. She came to me while I was preparing my Sunday dinner and took a seat at the kitchen table. She was depressed and was bemoaning the fact that she hadn't been a good mother to you. Anyway, she handed me this and told me she'd bought it on layaway at a jewelry store while working as a waitress in a restaurant. She wanted me to hold on to it and told me don't ever give it to her if she came asking for it. She told me to give it to you on a special day in your life. She wanted you to know she really did love you with all her heart in spite of the many times she disappointed you."

Sasha took the piece of jewelry and draped it over her hand and studied it in awe. "Why didn't you give it to me when I married Trey?"

Grandma Claudia pursed her lips. "I knew that mess of a marriage wasn't going to last. There was nothing special about that. Trey's parents were there looking on with disapproval, and he looked scared to death of what you two had to face with a child on the way. I had it in my purse, but I had a gut feeling that you were going to have better days. You worked so hard in everything you did. I was right not to give it to you. See, you can't mess with seasoned women. They can sense things that young folks don't have a clue about."

"You never mentioned how you felt back then. You and Granddad were always supportive of me and Trey."

"We certainly were. We were going to be there for you, right or wrong. That marriage is behind you, and you learned from it. Just think, you and

Trey have managed to even be friends for Craig's sake." She took the necklace from Sasha. "Hold still, so I can put this on you. I want you to remember your mother and all the good things you shared. I want you to remember how hard she tried to get on the right track because she loved you. She was a long way from being what any of us hoped or prayed she would be, but she was my baby girl, your mother. From your experiences, you know how hard it is to be a woman. Some of us have the courage to make it through, others stumble and fall too often in the name of love for that wrong man who comes along." She fastened the necklace. "How do you like it?"

Staring at herself in the mirror, Sasha touched the heart-shaped pendant gingerly. Her eyes brimmed with tears and she fell into her grandmother's arms. "She's here with me. I can feel it, Grandma."

"So can I, my dear. Her spirit is here to surround you with her love on the happiest day of your life. It is the perfect touch with your gown. Treasure that always. I hope you and Eric have a daughter you can pass it along to."

Suddenly, there was a knock on the door. Crystal, who had been putting the final touches on the bridesmaids' hair and makeup, opened the door. "Craig, my goodness, don't you look grown-up and fine?"

Dabbing her eyes carefully with tissues, Sasha said, "Come on in, son."

Craig strolled in, looking awkward and out of place around all the women there. He smiled when he saw his mother in her dress. "Mom, you look pretty." He leaned in and hugged her, careful not to muss her dress or makeup.

"Thank you, baby. Grandma, I'm going to cry again. Look at how handsome this young man is. Where is my little man?"

"Mom, don't do that. It's only the tux."

Crystal said, "Sasha, you have cried enough for everybody today, girl. Light that face up with a nice smile."

Everyone laughed at Crystal's efforts to ease Sasha's sentimental mood.

"The wedding planner says it's time for the ceremony to begin," Craig said, standing close to his mother so she could hear him among the talkative women.

Pam Hayes burst into the room out of breath, dressed in her bridesmaid outfit.

"I thought we were going to have to start without you," Sasha teased.

"I'm sorry I'm late. Blame my husband and his driving, okay?" Pam couldn't take her eyes off Sasha. "When Eric sees you coming down that aisle, you're going to take his breath away."

"That's my intention, girl."

The anxious wedding planner appeared at the door. "People, we want to begin on time. It's show-time. I want all of my bridesmaids to head to the vestibule of the church and line up. Grandma, you should be getting ready to be escorted down the aisle."

Grandma Claudia kissed Sasha and scurried away.

"Craig, wait exactly ten minutes before you bring your mother there. I'm counting on you to help her with her gown and all, but right now I want you to step into the hallway for a few minutes. Give your mother time to gather her thoughts. You can have only a couple of minutes alone, Sasha." The wedding planner closed the door.

Left all alone, Sasha was beginning to get the wedding jitters. She knew, though, the minute she looked into Eric's eyes she would be comforted, and the world would be right. She lowered her head and asked for God's blessings on this day.

There was a light knock on the door. It was the wedding planner. "It's time. Your groom is waiting for you." She smiled brightly. "Let's get going."

Taking a final look at herself, she sighed to relax and was on her way.

Sure enough, as she walked down the aisle on the arm of her tall, good-looking son and gazed at her man, with the sunlight highlighting him through the church window, she thought Eric looked like an angel.

When Sasha took her place at the altar beside Eric, she touched the heart pendant around her neck and lifted it to kiss it briefly. *I love you, Mom,* she thought. She gave Eric her hand and felt sparks of love as he squeezed it gently.

Sasha was overcome with joy as she and the man she planned to share a long life of love and abiding happiness with stood before the pastor. It was official. They were now Mr. and Mrs. Prince.